Elroy Greer has been having a really bad month. A co-worker blames him for mistakes he didn't make. His car is broken into. He lost most of his friends to his ex in the break-up. Then his hiking buddy bails at the last second, leaving Elroy alone at a trailhead. He decides some time in nature to get away from it all is still an excellent idea and heads out on his own. True to his bad luck, Elroy gets caught in a spring flash storm, loses his way, and tumbles off a cliff. He expects to die out there, but he doesn't. Elroy wakes up in a log cabin with a man who's already supposed to be dead — Rueben Calhoun. Except, Rueben is calling himself Dermot Reever. As Dermot begins explaining about wolf shifters and mates and that they are destined to be together, Elroy can hardly believe it's real. He's sure he'll wake up and find it's all been a pain-medicine-induced dream. If it's not a dream, can Elroy really take the chance that his bad luck won't ruin everything and have enough faith to begin a relationship with a wolf shifter in hiding?

This book is a work of fiction. Names, characters, places, and incidents either are products of the author's imagination or are used fictitiously. Any resemblance to actual events or locales or persons, living or dead, is entirely coincidental.

A Wolf in Hiding
Copyright © 2020 Charlie Richards
ISBN: 978-1-4874-2982-9
Cover art by Angela Waters

Published by eXtasy Books Inc or
Devine Destinies, an imprint of eXtasy Books Inc

Look for us online at:
www.eXtasybooks.com or www.devinedestinies.com

A Wolf in Hiding
Wolves of Stone Ridge Book 52

By

Charlie Richards

DEDICATION

To the readers who keep giving me new animals to turn into shift-ers. Thank you.

CHAPTER ONE

"**W**as anything stolen, sir?"

Elroy Greer barely managed to keep from rolling his eyes upon hearing the stupid question. Pointing at the gaping hole in the dash and dangling wires, he grumbled, "Do you mean other than the radio?"

The officer in blue lifted the hand holding his pen and made a placating gesture. "I didn't want to presume."

Feeling somewhat mollified, Elroy nodded. "Well, the radio was stolen as well as the change in my cup holder." He narrowed his eyes in thought. "It was maybe six bucks."

Sweeping his gaze over the interior of his *Jeep Grand Cherokee*, Elroy grimaced. His briefcase had been opened, and the contents were strewn over the back seat. Good thing he hadn't had any confidential files in it.

I'll remember never to leave my briefcase in my vehicle again.

Of course, how could Elroy have guessed that someone would break into his vehicle while he was eating lunch with Camilla? His best friend stood nearby, her arms crossed over her ample breasts. Her blonde brows were furrowed, and she nibbled her bottom lip.

Elroy had known Camilla Hudson since he was seven. They hadn't really become friends until they were twelve, though. He'd stopped a bully from pulling her hair on the playground, and they'd been inseparable ever since.

He hadn't even needed to tell her he was gay. Somehow, she'd just known. One day when they were both sixteen, she'd shocked the shit out of him by asking which boy he

1

planned to ask to the prom.

His parents, however, when Elroy had come out in college, they had disowned him. His younger brother and sister had done the same. Only his grandmother had stood at his side until she's passed away three years before.

When her will had been read, revealing everything had been put into a trust to be given to Elroy upon his thirtieth birthday, they'd tried to contest it. They were still trying, even after all this time. While Elroy didn't really need the money, he looked forward to turning thirty in four years only because it would mean an end to the court battles.

"Anything else, sir?" the cop pressed.

Rubbing his hands over his shortly cropped black hair, Elroy returned his attention to his *Cherokee*. "Uh, I had a CD case in here," he told the policeman. "I don't see it."

Elroy wasn't certain why a thief would take old CDs — maybe to pawn? Did pawn shops take CDs anymore? He'd switched to using playlists on his phone several years before.

Something else snagged Elroy's attention — or rather, the lack of something else. "Wait." He leaned into the vehicle and swished his hand through the center console. "Ah, fuck," he grumbled. Straightening, Elroy shoved his hands into his jacket pockets. "A three-eighty *Bodyguard* handgun. It was in the center console. I have a concealed carry permit."

"Can I see it, please, Mister Greer?"

Nodding, Elroy pulled out his phone. He opened an app and pulled up the document. Then he handed his phone to the cop.

The officer stared at the screen for a moment, then returned it to Elroy. "Was the gun registered in your name?"

Elroy nodded. "Yes, it was."

"Thank you, sir." The cop jotted a few words on his paperwork. "I'll get that reported as swiftly as possible. I'm sure your insurance will need a copy of my report, so if that's everything, I'll get started on it." The officer held out a card, and Elroy took it, seeing his name and number on it.

Insurance. Right. Another nightmare.

Nodding once more, Elroy returned his phone and the card to his jacket pocket. "Thank you."

"I'm sorry this happened, and I'll keep you updated if we get any luck on the prints."

After thanking the officer one more time, Elroy sighed and turned his attention back to his vehicle. At least it was Saturday, and he hadn't had to call in to work. He was already on his boss's shit list for something that wasn't his fault.

Fellow paralegal, Lane Peradu, had lied to Richmond Dessau and claimed Elroy had been the one doing the research on the Marcello case. In actuality, that had been one of Lane's cases, and no matter what the man said, he had not transferred it to Elroy. Lane had screwed up and missed information about their client's bank transactions. When the defendant—who was representing the husband in a messy divorce proceeding—had pointed out how the wife—who Richmond had been representing—had been slowly transferring funds from their joint account to a personal account for the last year, essentially stealing from her husband, the judge had not been impressed. Their client had not received the settlement she'd wanted, and Richmond had been understandably embarrassed.

Richmond had taken it out on Elroy, since he believed Lane, the senior paralegal by six months.

Elroy figured he was lucky he hadn't lost his job.

The bastard.

"I went inside and got some paper towels and a couple of cups of water from a waiter."

Upon hearing Camilla's voice, Elroy turned to face his friend. He smiled gratefully. "Thanks." He took the roll of towels from under her arm and tore off a couple of sheets. "I hadn't even thought about how to clean up the finger-printing powder."

After Elroy had been finger-printed to rule out his own, he'd used a wet nap that he'd had in the glove box—fortunately it had still been there and hadn't disappeared amidst the detritus littering his vehicle's seats and floors.

As they started cleaning up the powder, Camilla mused, "Who would pick your *Cherokee* when there are so many nicer cars in the lot?"

Elroy barked a laugh, mirth filling him. "Are you saying my baby's a POS?"

Camilla paused and gaped at him. "No!" Her cheeks pinked as she scowled at him. "I'm just saying that as I was walking back outside, I passed three cars with valuables easily seen through the window."

Humming, Elroy glanced around the lot. His bestie was right. The cars on the far side of the lot would have made better targets—more discreet. He'd parked close to the front, although the diners at the windows had claimed to have not seen anything.

"I see your point," Elroy admitted, frowning. "But I'm not a criminal, so I have no clue why someone would pick mine." Staring at his car, he muttered, "Maybe because there was obvious change in the cup holder?"

"Maybe." Camilla didn't sound convinced.

Elroy wadded up the damp paper towels and headed back toward the front of the restaurant and the garbage bin there. He tossed them, then stepped inside to return the remaining roll to the hostess. After receiving a commiserating smile from the petite brunette, he headed back outside.

Camilla continued to stand next to his car.

"I'm headed home to change, then meeting Bart at the Brine Falls trailhead," Elroy told her. He waved his hand toward the messy vehicle. "I'll clean up the rest of this tomorrow. Do you want to come?"

Shaking her head, Camilla bit her bottom lip as she rubbed her hands over her slightly rounded belly. She carried a bit of extra weight around her stomach and rear, and Elroy knew it made her self-conscious. He also knew she had a crush on Bart, which is why he'd invited her, even though he knew the outdoor activity wasn't really her thing.

"Um, no, thanks." Camilla shifted her weight from foot to foot as she admitted, "I don't want him to see me all blotchy and huffin' and puffin' while trying to climb that trail."

"Okay," Elroy conceded. "We'll pick a nature trail some time."

As one of his two remaining friends, he thought the pair would make a cute couple. Six months before, his ex-boyfriend of three years, Kyle, had left him. He'd boldly claimed that Elroy was a cold fish in bed on top of him working too much and not making time for him. Most of their mutual friends had chosen to stick with Kyle.

Bart had been the exception.

Elroy knew his buddy had just as big a crush on Camilla. They were just so damn shy...and oblivious. If Elroy hadn't been sworn to secrecy by both of them, they would already be together. Instead, they both pumped him for information about the other...and did nothing about it.

Gonna have to come up with some kind of plan.

"Call me if you want help cleaning out your car tomorrow," Camilla urged, stepping toward him and giving him a hug. "I don't have any plans except grocery shopping and laundry, and I can do those whenever."

After returning Camilla's hug, Elroy started toward the driver's door. "Thanks. I will," he replied. After one final wave, he climbed in and fired up his *Jeep*. At least having the stereo ripped out didn't mess up the engine.

Elroy waited until Camilla had made it to her car and

climbed in safely. Then he headed home. He changed from his nice jeans and top to something more suitable for climbing a mountain—older jeans, a sports polo, and hiking boots. Elroy gathered a couple of bottles of water, a pair of protein bars, some granola and jerky, and placed it all in a small backpack. Finally, he grabbed his jacket and headed out.

As Elroy drove, he shot off a text to Bart.

I'm headed out. What's your ETA?

Since Bart lived closer to the trailhead than Elroy did and they'd already planned to be there in the neighborhood of two PM, he figured his buddy would be waiting—probably with questions about his lunch with Camilla.

When Elroy didn't get a response right away, he placed his phone in the cup holder. He enjoyed the scenic drive along the winding roads, through the small town of Stone Ridge, and finally into the forested mountains. If his job hadn't been in the heart of Colin City, he would have bought a place closer to nature.

Elroy arrived at the trailhead and parked his car. To his surprise, he still hadn't heard from Bart. He picked up his phone, pleased to discover he still had a signal.

Dialing his friend's number, Elroy brought the phone to his ear.

"Hello?" Bart sounded distracted.

"Hey, Bart," Elroy greeted. "I'm at the trailhead, ready and waiting. When—"

Bart's cussing interrupted Elroy. "Ah, damn, man. I am so sorry." His tone held a wealth of regret and frustration. "Laura called in a panic because Nate crashed his bike and hurt himself, and Mark has the car for work. She needed a ride to take Nate to the hospital, and I…I shoulda called, but—" Groaning under his breath, Bart ran out of steam.

Even as disappointment flooded him, Elroy nodded in understanding. "It's okay, Bart. Really," he assured his friend. "Family comes first."

Elroy had met Bart's sister, Laura, on many occasions, and she was warm and accepting, not batting an eyelash when she discovered he was gay. Mark worked hard as an electrician, owning his own company, so it wasn't a surprise that he would work the occasional Saturday. Their ten-year-old son, Nate, was a great kid, if a little hyper at times.

After another deep sigh, Bart murmured, "I'm sorry I forgot to call you."

Leaning his head back against the headrest, Elroy closed his eyes. "Stop apologizing, Bart," he ordered, keeping his tone soothing. "Is Nate okay?"

"He will be. Sprained his right wrist."

"That won't slow him down for long." Elroy felt confident about that.

Bart chuckled softly. "You know it." After a couple of heartbeats of silence, he told him, "I'm still at the hospital. He should be discharged soon, but—"

"Hey. Relax, man." Elroy didn't care for the self-flagellation in Bart's tone. His buddy was too upbeat to sound so defeated. "We'll catch this trail another time."

"You're not goin' then?" Bart didn't let Elroy answer before adding, "Aren't you already there?"

"Yeah, but I've never hiked this trail before, and it's a strenuous one." Elroy didn't want to admit to being worried about hiking alone. "I think I'll head to Condor's Point trailhead and enjoy something a little more leisurely that I've done before."

"All right. Probably a good idea," Bart conceded. "We'll try for next weekend." He cleared his throat before saying, "Let me know how I can make it up to ya."

Elroy's first inclination was to reply, "Don't worry about it." Instead, he smiled. "You have plans for tomorrow afternoon?"

"Not currently."

An idea formed, and he grinned.

"You can come over and help me clean out my car." Elroy conveniently left out the part where Camilla would be there, too.

And I won't tell her, either.

If Elroy could get the pair working together for any length of time, he just knew they would get over their shyness and actually have a conversation, which could lead to a date.

"Sure, man," Bart replied. "You got it."

"Okay. I'll text you a time later," Elroy told him. "Go be with your family."

"Have a safe hike," Bart replied. "Bye."

"Later."

Elroy hung up, placed his phone in the cup holder, and re-started his engine. Then he headed toward the other trailhead.

Three hours later, Elroy decided Bart's order about having a safe hike had jinxed him. Pain radiated through his left leg, his right hand and wrist, and his head throbbed. He barely felt the shivers from the flash thunderstorm that had drenched him.

That's not good.

With his arms wrapped around his torso, Elroy sat on the wet ground and forced his eyelids open. He slowly panned his gaze over the forest around him. Then he peered up and behind him.

Breathing deeply, Elroy barely kept the spots dancing across his vision at bay.

Elroy had no idea where he was.

After getting turned around by the heavy rainstorm, making visibility next to nil, Elroy had figured hunkering down was his best option. He'd tried to search for a thicket or thick stand of trees to hide in. Instead, the undergrowth he'd chosen had hidden a cliff.

Between one step and the next, Elroy had fallen right over it.

When Elroy had landed, he'd screamed as his left leg snapped under him. He'd buckled, his right arm catching some of his weight and scraping over rocks. That pain caused him to twist, and he'd slammed his head against the cliff.

Elroy didn't know how he'd managed to stay conscious, but he'd done it. He slowly, carefully, eased to a sitting position, fighting the waves of nausea caused by the agony shooting through his leg. Having broken his arm once in the past, he recognized that kind of pain.

Leaning against the cliff face, Elroy panted softly. The spots increased even as the rain slacked off and stopped. Every shudder of his body brought fresh waves of debilitating throbs.

Elroy whimpered upon seeing the blood seeping through the left leg of his jeans. With a shaky left hand, he pulled his cell phone from his jacket pocket.

The cracked screen told him all he needed to know, but he tried waking it anyway.

Broken.

Taking a deep breath, Elroy used all his strength to bellow, "Hello?"

No answer.

Elroy gritted his teeth for several moments, then tried again.

Still nothing.

Unable to help himself, Elroy felt his eyes water as fear slithered through his veins.

"I'm gonna die out here," Elroy whispered, his heart clenching in his chest. The spots across his vision intensified as a wave of dizziness swept over him, caused by either blood loss or fear. He wasn't certain which.

Movement to his right caught his attention, and he blinked, barely able to focus on it.

"No way," Elroy mumbled as his heart rate spiked for a new reason.

A medium brown and tan wolf padded toward him.

At least I won't die of exposure.

That was Elroy's last thought as he gave in to the pain, and his eyes rolled to the back of his head as he passed out.

CHAPTER TWO

The mixture of agony and fear in the human's voice had called to Dermot Reever on a visceral level. Running back toward his cabin in wolf form, intending to get out of the sudden spring downpour, he'd immediately changed directions. The canyon made pinpointing the source of the call difficult, but Dermot was determined.

When the masculine cry of *hello* came again, Dermot had a second point of reference, aiding him in his search.

The rain had stopped by the time Dermot reached the human, and the scent of his blood perfumed the air. The delicious aroma caused him to salivate. He wanted to lick the human's wounds and give him pleasure.

Mate!

The word reverberated through Dermot's instinct-driven brain, and excitement flooded him.

So did arousal.

For the first time in almost a hundred years, Dermot popped a boner in wolf form.

Damn, he smells good!

Except, considering the heaviness of the iron-rich scent, Dermot realized his mate must have lost a lot of blood.

Get your head out of your ass, Dermot!

Padding toward the human, Dermot spotted the instant the guy's eyes rolled to the back of his head. He lunged forward, barely managing to get his furry body under the man's torso before he smacked his head on a rock. From the smell of his blood originating from different locations, Dermot figured his

11

mate had already done that once.

Ever-so-carefully, Dermot slithered sideways, lowering his mate gently to the ground. When he didn't even moan, a healthy dose of worry slammed into him.

Dermot backed up a step and shifted. His muscles popped, bones crackled, and his skin rippled. After a handful of heartbeats, he peered at his mate with human eyes for the first time.

Unfortunately, Dermot didn't have time to admire the human's medium-brown skin or toned and lean runner's build. The amount of blood soaked into his mate's left lower leg, as well as it's slightly unnatural angle, told Dermot where most of the fragrance was coming from. He gently lifted the man's arms away from his torso, searching for any other injuries that would make moving him difficult.

To Dermot's relief, the only other blood he found was seeping from a gash on the flesh of his right hand and wrist. Even the blood on the back of his head had clotted. When he gently moved his hands along the man's torso and ribcage, everything was firm and as it should be.

Gods, I wish I were feeling up my mate for an entirely different reason.

Even as the thought entered Dermot's mind, he dismissed it.

Get my mate to safety and to medical attention. Then I can dream of fucking and claiming him.

"Let's get you out of here, handsome," Dermot crooned. "But how to do that?"

Dermot knew the area, having run through it as a wolf for over a hundred years. The area he was in was rocky with rough terrain between the cliff and his cabin. Carrying him as a human would tear up his feet, but he couldn't get him out as a wolf, either.

Loath to leave his mate—even for the forty minutes it would take to sprint home, call in the help of his pack-mates, then sprint back again—he searched for another option.

Spotting the hiking boots on the human's feet, Dermot considered them.

Close enough.

Dermot removed his man's hiking boots, then shoved his own feet into them. They were a size too small, but he could deal with that. Crouching, he slipped his arms under his man and lifted him.

Straightening, Dermot spotted a backpack ten feet away, so he crossed to it and snagged it with the hand running under his mate's torso.

As swiftly and as carefully as he could, he hurried home.

Over forty-five minutes later — the trip took much longer in human form, but at least they'd made it — Dermot strode into his cabin. His retreat was a one-bedroom with indoor plumbing and a large claw-footed tub. He had all the modern amenities, even though he was hiding out in the woods for the next decade or more.

I hope my mate likes it.

The idea of the human in his arms spending hours exploring the mountains with him brought a smile to his lips.

Gotta woo him first.

Chuckling under his breath, Dermot entered his bedroom. *Our bedroom, now.* He settled his mate on the mattress before rushing out again.

Dermot grabbed his cell phone and punched *three* on speed dial. As he listened to the line ring, he tucked the phone between his ear and shoulder and hurried around the cabin. He had a rudimentary idea of what was needed, so he started the kitchen faucet, turning the water to hot.

As Dermot gathered towels from the kitchen and bathroom, the line picked up.

"Greetings, Dermot. How are ye fairin'? Need help with something?"

Upon hearing his alpha's deep, Irish-accented voice, Dermot felt himself settle. He hadn't even realized he'd been that nervous. Finding his mate injured after what appeared to be a fall off a cliff had rattled him more than he'd realized.

"I do need help with something, Alpha Declan. Thank you for taking my call."

"I'm always happy to assist me pack members, Dermot," Alpha Declan told him, warmth filling his tone. "What's up?"

After grabbing the scissors from the butcher block, Dermot started carrying everything back to the bedroom. His mate hadn't moved.

"I found my mate while running in the mountains," Dermot revealed. "He was a hiker."

"Grand!" Alpha Declan cried, clearly pleased. "Not the best timing, but we'll help ye win her...or him. What trail-head, and what does yer mate look like? I assume ye followed him or her down the mountain, so we have somethin' to go on?"

"It's a he, and he was injured after falling off a cliff," Dermot hurriedly explained as he began carefully removing his mate's soaked jacket. "I need the alpha-mate, please. His left leg is broken. There's a lot of blood. I—" A fissure of fear worked through Dermot. "He's unconscious, and I'm getting him out of his soaked clothes, but he's still not waking up, and I—"

"Take a deep breath, Dermot," Alpha Declan encouraged, his tone a deep croon. "Where are ye?"

"My cabin."

As soon as those words were out of his mouth, Dermot did as he'd been told. He took several slow deep breaths. While Dermot did that, he heard his alpha shout Lark's name.

Lark Trystan was a small, blond human. Most would call him a twink. His personality was vivacious and friendly, and he complemented the alpha's serious demeanor perfectly. He was also a doctor.

"What are you yelling about?" Lark asked, amusement in his tone.

Dermot's heightened shifter hearing easily allowed him to hear what those on the other end of the line were saying.

Alpha Declan quickly relayed what Dermot had shared.

"Tell me about his injuries," Lark demanded, his voice now coming clearly through the line. He must have taken the phone from Declan. "At least, what you can see."

After sharing what he'd discovered, he listened to Lark tell Declan what to pack.

During that time, Dermot put the phone on speaker and placed it on the nearby pillow. He picked up the scissors and cut his human's shirt off. He just about swallowed his tongue upon seeing all the gorgeous milk-chocolate skin spread out on his bed. Doing his best to ignore his randy dick, he eased his arm under the man's torso and lifted so he could pull the wet shirt out from under him.

Finally, Dermot grabbed a towel and began rubbing his human's skin. Once his torso was dry, he spread a quilt over him. He turned his attention to the man's wet jeans, but he hesitated, uncertain what he'd find under the fabric of his left leg.

"Should I leave his jeans on?" Dermot asked, cutting into whatever Lark had been telling Declan. "They're soaked from the rain, but with his broken leg, I'm worried about making it worse."

"Remove what you can, but leave the left leg to me," Lark ordered. "I'll walk you through cleaning and bandaging his hand, wrist, and head. Got it?"

Dermot nodded, blowing out a relieved breath.

"Bet you just nodded, right?" Lark asked, his voice containing just a hint of teasing.

"Yeah. Sorry."

Dermot felt his cheeks heat a little, and he rubbed a hand through his damp hair, pushing the shaggy locks away from his face. That was about the time he realized he was still naked. His sore feet reminded him that his mate's hiking boots were a size too small.

After toeing off the boots, Dermot grabbed a pair of sweatpants out of his dresser. He yanked them on before returning to the bed. Then he started the process of cutting off his mate's jeans.

Dermot removed the right leg and crotch, revealing navy-blue briefs. Damp or not, he left those on. Ever-so-carefully, he started cutting down the human's left leg. He stopped mid-thigh.

After Dermot gently removed his socks, he dried the exposed flesh. Finally, he spread the throw blanket over the rest of him, hoping it would help warm him.

"Okay. I'm done with the pants," Dermot announced before he discovered he could hear the rumble of an engine through the line. Relief filled him a little more, since that told him Declan and Lark were en route. "Should I start with his hand or head?"

"Head," Lark told him.

Over the course of the next thirty minutes, Dermot followed Lark's precise instructions.

Just as Dermot was finishing up with the bandage to his human's hand and wrist—he'd even managed to put a few stitches in him—his sensitive hearing caught the whine of an approaching engine.

"You here?"

"Yes," Lark confirmed. "Open your door."

Dermot rushed from the room to obey. He threw open the front door and watched as a large SUV skidded to a stop. His alpha shoved from the driver's side and jumped out.

"Come help," Alpha Declan ordered, turning toward the

back, which was already opening.

Obeying, Dermot jogged to the rear of the vehicle. He spotted a bunch of electronic equipment and a couple of bags. He grabbed the handles of a bag in each hand and headed toward his cabin.

His alpha followed with a box-like contraption.

Dermot hurried back to the bedroom and spotted Lark already there. The alpha-mate leaned over his human's head. He had a pen-light in his hand and was holding his mate's eyelid open as he shone it into it.

"What's his name?" Lark asked in an absent manner while starting to go through some other checks that Dermot didn't understand.

"Uhhhhh."

Turning to the remnants of his mate's discarded jeans, Dermot picked them up. While he'd noticed the bulge of the wallet, he hadn't bothered to look at it. He tugged it from one of the back ones and opened it.

Finding the human's driver's license was easy enough.

Dermot read, "Elroy Greer."

Even just saying the name out loud caused a slither of heat to bloom in Dermot's gut. The arousal that he'd been beating back while aiding his mate surged anew. His blood flowed south, and his dick plumped behind his sweats…which would hide nothing.

Considering a shifter's heightened sense of smell could detect arousal, it really didn't matter.

"I'm going to cut off his left jeans, so I can do X-rays and see what I'm working with," Lark told him as he inspected the bandages Dermot had put on Elroy. He straightened as he turned to face him. "It's highly likely that this will hurt him. If you can't control yourself, I'm going to need you to leave."

Dermot opened his mouth, then closed it again. Turning, he grabbed a nearby chair and dragged it to the left side of the bed, up by Elroy's head. He plopped onto it, then gently cradled Elroy's left hand between both of his own.

Lark took that as his answer and began cutting off the remaining jeans.

Doing his best to ignore what was going on to his left, Dermot leaned forward. "Hi, Elroy," he purred into the unconscious man's ear. "My name's Dermot Reever. I am so sorry you were injured, but I'm also very happy to have met you." Moving his right hand to Elroy's forehead, Dermot skimmed his fingertips along his human's scalp. "I can't wait to hold you and care for you as you heal. I'll take ever-so-good care of you, my mate."

"Hold the X-ray machine a little to the left, Declan," Lark ordered, catching Dermot's attention.

Dermot spotted the torn flesh and jut of bone between the flaps on the left side of Elroy's calf. Grimacing, he sucked in a harsh breath, doing his best to ignore the roll of his stomach. Yanking his gaze away from the grotesque sight, he refocused on his mate's face.

"Let me tell you, Elroy," Dermot murmured, doing his best to once again ignore what Lark and Declan were doing. "I'm real happy you're sleeping through this. That looks beyond disgusting." Forcing a soft chuckle, he admitted, "I was in the military for over a decade, and I never could get used to the sight of torn flesh." He lowered his voice and whispered, "I faked it real good, but I'll certainly never have the makings for a doctor in one of my upcoming lives."

As a shifter—a paranormal being that could live upward of five hundred years—he had to recreate his identity every few decades. That was why he was hiding out in the mountains right then. He needed those humans who knew him to forget who he was, leave the area, or die.

A low groan rumbled from Elroy.

Dermot jerked his attention to Elroy's face, seeing movement behind the lids.

"Easy, now, Elroy," Dermot rumbled, gently massaging his hand as well as his temple. "You're safe. You'll be okay. We'll take real good for you."

As Dermot watched, Elroy's eyelids fluttered. He held his breath, and his heart pounded in his chest. Anticipation flooded him as he waited to catch his first sight of Elroy's eyes.

"Come on, baby," Dermot encouraged. "Open them peepers. Look at me."

Elroy's pupils were heavily dilated when he finally turned his head and focused on him. Then his beautiful brown eyes widened. "Rueben?" he said on a gasp. "Rueben Calhoun?"

"Uh…" Dermot struggled with how to respond. "Y-You know me?"

"You're dead," Elroy whispered roughly. "Am I dead, too?"

"You're not dead, baby," Dermot assured.

Elroy glanced down his body, obviously focusing on his leg. "Oh!" Then his eyes rolled, and he passed back out.

"Well, that creates a bit of a hiccup," Declan rumbled, drawing Dermot's attention. "He recognized ye from yer old life. Ye don't remember this man?"

Dermot shook his head. "No." Returning his focus to Elroy, he mused, "So how do you know me, baby?"

CHAPTER THREE

Images flashed across the backs of Elroy's eyelids as his mind floated on a sea of white noise.

Meds. I'm on meds.

Elroy hated meds. He liked a clear head.

So why would I take them?

Struggling to push through the fog enough to focus, Elroy considered the hazy memories.

Hiking. Rain. Falling.

Agony!

Sucking in a harsh breath, Elroy snapped his eyelids open…or he tried to. They felt gummy, and it was tough. After lifting his right arm, he attempted to wipe them. A soft fabric scratched over his skin instead.

Then Elroy remembered it wasn't just his left leg that had sustained injury. Someone must have bandaged his sliced palm and wrist. He wondered how they'd saved him from the wolf.

Holy shit. I didn't even know there were wolves in these mountains.

Elroy always carried bear spray while out hiking, but it had been attached to his backpack. He didn't know where that had ended up after his fall. Oddly enough, even disoriented, he felt warm and comfortable.

Except, I don't hear the beeps of machines, like in a hospital.

There was no smell of antiseptic, either.

Where am I?

Lifting his left hand, Elroy managed to massage his eyes,

swiping away the crusties. He had to blink a few times to get his eyes to focus, but he managed it. What he saw didn't answer any of his questions, though.

Elroy lay in a bed—a real soft one—in a bedroom that looked, well, rustic. There were wood walls like a cabin. The dresser and nightstands were made of some knotty wood. Even the door to the closet appeared...

Did a hunter find me and take me to their cabin?

"Hi, Elroy. I was beginning to worry."

The deep voice drew Elroy's attention to the other side of the room.

Gasping, Elroy gaped. He'd dismissed that memory—no way could it have been real. Except, there he was, slowly moving toward him, carrying a tray containing a bowl, a couple of mugs, and some cutlery.

"Rueben," Elroy murmured. "Y-You're alive."

How can this be? Are the meds making me hallucinate?

Nodding, Rueben set the tray on a second dresser. "I'm not a hallucination."

Crap. I said that out loud.

Then Rueben picked up a steaming mug and a spoon. "And I'll explain, but how about some tea first." He settled on a chair by the bed to his left. "I thought I'd have to force-feed you the pain meds again, so I had them dissolve in this mug."

"No meds," Elroy countered, trying to push away the spoonful of liquid Rueben was extending toward his mouth. He swallowed convulsively, wishing he could get some water.

Rueben placed the spoon in the mug, then balanced it on his thigh. Leaning toward Elroy, he peered at him with his penetrating brown eyes. "You have a compound fracture of your left tibia and a straight break in your fibula. You need pain meds."

"Too strong," Elroy whispered. "Don't like how they feel."

"I'm with you on that, so I understand, Elroy," Rueben told

him. "But in about fifteen minutes, the dose I gave you four hours ago is going to wear off, and you're going to end up in agony." His dark brows furrowed, and his features tightened. "I don't want to see you like that."

Elroy groaned even as he thought about that. His tolerance for pain was pretty damn high, but he didn't want to think about how that had come about. Plus, no way would he explain it to a stranger who was supposed to be dead.

Even if he is a sexy as fuck stranger who I lusted after from afar for over two months.

"How about a half dose?" Rueben offered suddenly. He stood and headed back to the dresser where a small pill bottle rested. "It'll take the edge off, I think. Then you can decide if you need more or less."

Sighing, Elroy nodded. "Okay."

Rueben smiled as he opened it. "Good." He shook a very small white tablet into his palm, then closed the bottle. "I'll cut this in half, and you can swallow it."

Putting word to deed, Rueben grabbed a sheathed knife and pulled it free. He placed the pill on the dresser, then cut it in half. After putting the knife down, he picked up the pill, the second mug, and returned to him.

"Open your mouth," Rueben instructed.

Elroy obeyed.

With a smile, Rueben popped it into Elroy's mouth. Then he cradled his nape and lifted him a little. He held the mug to his lips, urging him to drink.

The soothing coolness of water spread over Elroy's tongue. He moaned softly as he swallowed, gulping greedily. When Rueben began to pull it away, he instinctively reached to keep it close.

"Easy, Elroy," Rueben rumbled, his voice holding a deep croon. "You'll get more soon. I have broth, too. Let's get some of that down you."

"If you didn't know I was awake, why make it?" Elroy

asked curiously, returning his hands to the blanket covering him.

Rueben winked. "Wishful thinking."

Something else stuttered through Elroy's sluggish brain. "Guess I should have asked before, but…what was that you gave me?"

After picking up the bowl and grabbing a fresh spoon, Rueben paused and tilted his head. His eyes narrowed. "Hmm, now that I think about it, I don't think Lark told me." With a shrug, he returned to Elroy's side. "Do you want me to help you sit up, so you can drink this yourself?" Rueben smiled as heated light entered his eyes. "Although, I've enjoyed it plenty to feed you these last coupla days."

Alarm flooded Elroy…and it stemmed from so many sources.

"Oh, god. Lark? That sounds like a hippie name," Elroy blurted out. Staring at Rueben, wide-eyed, he couldn't help the squeak in his voice as he asked, "You're not giving me an illicit substance, are you? You were a lawyer, Rueben. Why would you do that to me? I—" Then a tremble worked through him, and he scowled at the comforter. "Couple of days? Oh, shit!"

"Whoa, whoa, Elroy." Rueben was suddenly there on the bed beside him, wrapping him in his arms. "You're okay, my mate. Take deep breaths." He nuzzled his bearded lips against Elroy's temple. "I would never do anything to hurt you. You're safe."

Elroy clutched at Rueben's flannel shirt. Clinging to the near-stranger, he inhaled deeply, doing as he'd been bidden. The man smelled of wood-smoke and fresh air, pine, and something else…something masculine that enflamed Elroy's senses even as it calmed him.

"That's the way," Rueben purred into his ear before licking

the sensitive skin behind it. "You're fine. I'll explain every-thing." He suckled Elroy's lobe, drawing a gasp from him, then added, "Gods, I love holding you."

Truth be told, Elroy was loving being held by Rueben. He didn't say that, however. His senses were all over the place, and he didn't trust them. Plus, Elroy thought it might be be-cause Kyle had dumped him almost six months ago, and he hadn't gotten any action since…being held or otherwise.

"So, first," Rueben began. "Lark is not a hippie. Lark is Doctor Lark Trystan. He used to work at Sugar Creek Memo-rial, but he opened his own private practice a few years ago." Rueben drew back just a little, using his hold on Elroy's jaw to encourage him to meet his gaze. "He and a paramedic, Manon Lemelle, performed surgery on your leg to patch it to-gether, and they casted it. They would never give you some-thing illegal. I just didn't bother to ask what it was, because I trust them."

Then Rueben swept his gaze over Elroy's blanket-covered form. When he returned his focus to Elroy's eyes, he could see the heat in them. His bearded lips curved into a wicked smile.

"And you're going to be off your feet for some time," Rue-ben told him. "So you're in my home so I can take care of you."

Elroy nodded as his body began to sluggishly respond to Rueben's expression. How he'd dreamed of being noticed by that man…before his death. Even more confusion filled him.

How did Rueben end up being reported as dead, and why was he living in a cabin? His appearance had certainly changed, too. Gone were the eyebrow piercings as well as the clean-shaven look. Rueben had grown his hair out, and it reached his shoulders in thick waves. Plus, he sported a closely-trimmed beard.

I've never been attracted to a guy with facial hair before, but damn does it look good on him.

And this is not what I should be focusing on.

Damn meds messing with me some more.

Elroy dragged his mind back to where it needed to be...figuring out his situation. He didn't recognize the doctor's name, but that didn't mean anything. He'd never had cause to go to Sugar Creek Memorial.

And on that note...

"Why wasn't I taken to the hospital?" Elroy frowned at the bigger man in confusion. "Two days. Was I reported missing?"

"First, yes, you were reported missing on Sunday afternoon by a woman named Camilla," Reuben told him. The lust disappeared from his eyes, and his lips pinched. "Is she someone special to you? Girlfriend?"

"Best friend," Elroy replied. Squinting up at Rueben, he asked, "Are you jealous?" Wincing, Elroy muttered, "I can't believe I said that out loud."

Rueben chuckled softly. "You're a lightweight. Good thing we switched to halves, huh?" Then his attention slid to his casted leg. "How's your leg feel? Pain tolerable?"

Elroy glanced at his leg, taking in the way it was propped up on pillows. A pale blue cast covered him from mid-thigh to his foot. A sock had been pulled over his toes, probably to keep them warm.

To Elroy's surprise, he hadn't even noticed the dull ache pulsing through his leg until Rueben had made him focus on it.

"I'm okay," Elroy assured. Turning his attention to his right hand, he lifted it. "And this?"

While gently scraping his fingertips over his short hair along his nape, Rueben told him, "You sprained it while putting an impressive tear in your palm and up the inside of your wrist about three inches." His smile appeared reassuring even as he continued, "Only seven stitches. Fortunately, once we bond, that will heal pretty swiftly."

Huh?

"Bond?"

Rueben's cheeks darkened enough that it managed to show through his beard. "Sorry. Haven't gotten to that part of the explanation, yet." Scoffing, he offered Elroy a wry grin. "It's part of why you weren't taken to the hospital, and why we can't have you speaking with Camilla or Bart, yet."

"Do they still think I'm lost, Rueben?" Elroy asked in alarm.

"No." Rueben shook his head once. "And I really need you to stop calling me Rueben. He died in October of last year." His dark eyes intense, he claimed, "I'm Dermot Reever now, and I need you to start calling me that."

Elroy opened his mouth, then shut it just as quickly. Finally, he squeaked, "Wh-What are you talking about, Rueben?"

Rueben's lips tightened into a thin line. "Dermot. Please say it."

"D-Dermot," Elroy whispered obediently.

"Dermot Reever."

Elroy gulped before parroting Rueben — Dermot. "Dermot Reever."

"Thank you, Elroy. I know you don't understand, but this is important." Rueben — Dermot rubbed his thumb along Elroy's jawline, sending delicious tingles down his neck. "Right now, Camilla thinks you're in a cabin with the park ranger who found you. The rainstorm created a rockslide, and we're currently trapped." Dermot teased that same thumb along Elroy's lower lip. "Once everything is explained and you have accepted your new reality, you can see her again. I hear Bart is with her, keeping her calm. People in my pack are monitoring. You can even use a radio phone to talk to her soon, once explanations are done."

Taking in the heated expression on Dermot's face as he continued to trace over Elroy's features, the dull ache in his leg began to be beaten out by a different kind of throb. His blood flowed south, causing his dick to stiffen. He felt his heart pound in his chest as a desire to beg for a kiss swelled within him.

"Oh, baby," Dermot whispered on a groan. "I love the way you're looking at me, and I want to kiss you so damn badly. May I?"

Elroy stared up at the man in bed beside him. Before the guy's death, he had fantasized about this sort of thing happening. Well, not the broken leg part, but he'd wanted Dermot to notice him, to pursue him.

At the time, Elroy had felt guilty as hell about it, since he'd been in a relationship.

Except now, I'm not.

There were still so many questions Elroy needed answers to, but with his body beginning to burn with desire and his fantasy man holding him in his arms and all but begging to kiss him, Elroy couldn't help himself.

"Yes."

With a groan, Dermot lowered his head and sealed his lips over Elroy's. The man teased his tongue along his lower lip, and he immediately opened to him. Elroy welcomed Dermot's tongue, happy to slide his own along it.

Dermot's masculine flavor burst across his senses. He tasted of coffee, a sweetener, and something inherently all Dermot. While Elroy had never cared for coffee, he suddenly found the flavor okay when on Dermot's tongue.

Sliding his left hand up, Elroy threaded it through Dermot's thick hair. He found the strands soft, pleasing to touch. Cradling Dermot's head, he tilted his own just a little and deepened the kiss, pushing his tongue into the other man's mouth.

Feeding him a growl, Dermot met him thrust for thrust as their appendages dueled.

Fire coursed through Elroy's body as he gave as good as he

got. His cock ached beneath the blanket. He began to shift his hips restlessly while moving his bandaged hand to his groin, searching for pressure.

Pain exploded up his left leg.

Gasping, Elroy tore his lips away from the other man's mouth. He turned his head and moaned...and not the good kind. At the same time, his hand in Dermot's hair clenched.

Dermot grunted, probably from Elroy yanking his hair.

As spots danced across Elroy's vision, he sucked in a noisy breath, struggling to breathe for more than one reason.

"Shit, baby. I'm so sorry," Dermot rumbled, petting his face, neck, and chest. "I shouldn't have let that get so out of hand. I just—Gods, you're so fucking sexy. I—" Dermot groaned again as he continued to touch Elroy, obviously trying to soothe him.

"It's okay," Elroy managed to say on panting breaths. Forcing his eyelids open, he smiled wryly at a worried-looking Dermot. "Never felt anything like that from a kiss before. Went right to my little head." Appreciating that his dark skin would hide his blush, Elroy admitted, "When admiring you in the halls of the courthouse, I sure never expected chemistry like this."

Dermot's expression sobered a little even as he returned Elroy's smile. "Can't believe you were in the courthouse, and I missed you. Damn." Then he shook his head as he added, "And we have explosive chemistry because we're mates, Elroy."

Recalling Dermot calling him his mate once before, Elroy asked, "What's that mean?"

After taking a deep sigh, as if gearing himself up for something, Dermot let it out between pursed lips. "Elroy, I am a wolf shifter. A paranormal being that can turn into a wolf at will."

Dermot rubbed his palm over Elroy's chest, perhaps attempting to soothe after such an outlandish proclamation, but he didn't stop there.

"You are my mate. The other half of my soul. The one person on this earth that I can bond with and share my hundreds year-long life with."

It finally clicked.

Cocking his head, Elroy murmured, "They were going to commit you, so you faked your death and ran away to the mountains, didn't you?"

Damn. Why were all the hotties either taken or crazy?

CHAPTER FOUR

Dermot hadn't expected Elroy to believe him, but that was okay. The natural human reaction was to deny. After all, most humans didn't know about the paranormal world.

That will change, my mate.

Staring fondly at Elroy, Dermot chuckled softly. "Don't believe me. That's okay." He shook his head slowly as he took in Elroy's incredulous expression. "Humans rarely do when they're first told that paranormals live and work right beside them."

When Elroy continued to stare at him as if he had two heads, Dermot eased away from him. He rose to a sitting position on the bed. Holding his mate's gaze, he cocked his head as he thought quickly.

"Do you remember the wolf that found you after the storm?" Dermot asked, hoping Elroy still retained his memories.

Elroy's eyes narrowed. "Yes." He rubbed his left hand over the bandage on his right. "I thought he was going to eat me."

Dermot shook his head. "Never. That wolf was me." Lifting his hand when he saw Elroy open his mouth, he hurried to say, "When I'm in my wolf form, I am completely cognizant. I know who people are, and I can think and reason just as when I'm in my human form."

"I don't believe you."

Upon hearing Elroy's denial, Dermot hummed. "Again, I'm not surprised. Humans like proof, and I'll give it to you."

Scoffing, Elroy rolled his eyes.

"Never been interested in the paranormal, huh?"

Dermot had to smirk upon seeing Elroy's scowl. The furrowing of his brows created a crease above his nose that he found cute. He kept the thought to himself, however, figuring Elroy wouldn't appreciate his admiration at the moment.

Elroy sighed deeply. "I don't understand how you can think you can give me proof." Gripping Dermot with his good hand, he squeezed his wrist. "If you want to live in a fantasy in your head out here in the middle of the woods, go for it. Hell, you're not hurting anybody, so—" Elroy shrugged. "I won't tell anyone you're alive, so whoever was after you will continue to leave you alone."

Huh. Isn't that sweet of him.

Winking, Dermot rested his other hand over Elroy's hand. "Thank you, my mate. It's very considerate of you. However"—he held up one finger to stall Elroy's reply—"I was telling you about what happens while in wolf form, so you didn't freak out and try to jump off the bed. I don't want you to reinjure yourself just so you'll believe me." Then Dermot drew away. "I would never hurt you, so please don't do anything to hurt yourself."

Elroy's eyes were narrowed as Dermot rose to his feet. Knowing there wasn't much else he could say, he opened the top couple of buttons on his flannel shirt. Then he tugged it over his head.

As Dermot dropped it on the chair, he heard Elroy gasp. When he spotted his mate's focus riveted on his chest, he had to grin. Lifting his hand, Dermot skimmed it over his pierced nipple, giving the small silver hoop a slight tug.

"Like these?" Dermot asked. He couldn't help the way his voice deepened. The appreciative gleam in his mate's eyes caused a flash of smug heat to flood his veins.

Elroy licked his lips, then swallowed hard enough to cause his Adam's apple to bob. "N-Never really thought about piercings before."

Dermot arched one brow as he slipped his thumbs into the waistband of his sweatpants. "Really?" Then he pulled them forward and down, allowing his erection to swing free. "Never?"

As Dermot shoved his sweats off with one hand, he gripped his shaft with the other. He teased his fingertips over the balls of the jacob's ladder running along the underside of his cock while using his thumb to flick the prince albert's hoop. Dermot had a guiche piercing behind his balls, but he would have to show that one off another time.

"Oh, wow," Elroy whispered.

The sight of Elroy's wide eyes sent a burst of flames through Dermot's blood, and he couldn't help the low moan from slipping from him. Nor could he stop the bead of pre-cum from oozing from his slit. Growling softly, he rubbed it into his glans before he managed to tear his hand away from his dick.

"Fucking hell, Elroy," Dermot grumbled. "Everything about you is distracting the hell out of me."

Elroy's attention snapped to Dermot's face. Even with his dark skin, he could see his flush. His mate's renewed arousal perfuming the air didn't help his randy state, either.

"Y-You're the one who just got naked," Elroy commented huskily. He moved his hand to his crotch, showcasing the tented blanket. "Wh-Why would you d-do that?"

Why indeed?

Right.

Dermot drew in a steadying breath…which didn't really help, considering the pheromones flooding the bedroom.

Gods, my mate is in my bed. I —

Groaning for a new reason, Dermot shook his head as he backed up a step. "I-I'm going to shift. Show you my wolf." After another step backward, his butt bumping into his dresser, he lifted a hand in warning. "It sounds worse than it is, so just stay calm and stay in bed."

Elroy's expression proved he still didn't believe him.

He will, though.

Dermot crouched and called to his wolf. Being aroused so deeply, it took him a bit longer than normal to work through his change. He eventually managed it.

Finally, Dermot opened his eyes and peered at Elroy.

His mate's jaw was gaping, and his eyes were wide. He clutched the blanket in both hands to his chest as if it was a shield. Every visible line of his body showcased his tension.

It was the scent of fear filling the air that concerned Dermot the most.

Damn it.

Lowering to his belly, Dermot whined softly. He crept forward a couple of steps, wanting to get nearer so he could soothe his mate. That only drew a whimper from Elroy.

Dermot racked his brain for a way to connect. If he could have rolled his eyes in canine form, he would have.

Of course.

Lifting his butt in the air, Dermot wagged his tail and yipped, giving a classic friendly doggy greeting. Then he flopped over and rolled to his back. Wriggling on the floor, he kicked up his legs, batting the air playfully.

"Holy fucking shit. Rue, uh, Dermot?"

Dermot rolled back over and sat up. He tilted his head and whined softly.

"Is that really you?" Elroy's eyes were still wide, but the stench of fear was dissipating. "How is this possible?"

Returning to his belly, Dermot crept forward. He made it to the side of the bed, then rested his head on it. Dermot whined again before rubbing his cheek on the blanket.

"This is unbelievable. If I hadn't seen it..." Elroy slowly released the death grip he had on the comforter. He lifted his hand and began reaching toward him, then paused. "C-Can I, uh, touch you?"

Dermot lifted his head and bobbed it in a nod. Then he

flicked out his tongue and licked Elroy's palm. To Dermot's relief, that drew a chuckle from his mate.

After a few more heartbeats, Elroy closed the distance between his hand and his furry head. He rubbed his palm over Dermot's coat, rubbing and ruffling his fur. When Elroy scratched at his ear, Dermot groaned in pleasure and pressed into his touch.

So, so good.

Elroy explored his head, neck, and ruff for several minutes before drawing away. "Okay, um. I have questions." Furrowing his brows, he asked, "Can you change back at will, or do you have to remain like that for a certain length of time? H-How does that work?"

Beyond ecstatic that Elroy had accepted his wolf, Dermot took a few steps backward. He reached for his human form and shifted. Then he rose to his feet and peered at his still wide-eyed mate.

"I have complete control over my form," Dermot told him, moving back to the bed. "The moon doesn't rule us or anything like that."

Seeing Elroy's focus drift downward, Dermot bit back a growl of delight. His mate was once again staring at his groin. He couldn't very well do anything about his engorged shaft unless he jacked off, which would only be a temporary fix.

"See something you like?" Dermot rumbled gruffly. "Should I get dressed?"

Dermot prayed to the gods that Elroy said no. He knew for a fact that his mate only wore briefs under that blanket. His pack-mates had brought a brand new package of them, and Dermot had changed them out twice.

I know exactly what his gorgeous cock and balls look like…soft, anyway.

"I-I…I think I have some qu-questions, and I—" Elroy lifted his gaze to Dermot. "But, god, I want you to fuck me with that thing."

Dermot groaned and grabbed his cock. His balls began to lift as a tingle started at the base of his spine. He squeezed the base, barely able to stem his orgasm.

If just Elroy's husky voice and pleading for a fucking could set him off, he worried he wouldn't be able to control himself long enough to give his soon-to-be lover what he wanted.

"I can't fuck you like I want to with your leg like that, baby," Dermot murmured as he drew closer. "And you've been lying in my bed for two days. If I roll you on your side, slot up behind you, and sink into your sweet heat, be warned, I will claim you."

Just saying the words caused his heart to hammer in his chest, and his gut clenched. Pre-cum bubbled from his slit. He squeezed the base of his prick harder.

"Wh-What's claiming?"

Right. Basic shifter one-oh-one.

Clearing his throat, Dermot forced himself to sit on the clothes he'd left on the chair. The bowl of broth he'd set on the nightstand when Elroy had begun to freak out caught his attention. He grabbed it and held it out to his mate.

"Drink as I explain."

To Dermot's pleasure, Elroy took the bowl in his left hand. He settled it on his stomach, then frowned at it.

Dermot realized his predicament. Leaning forward, he slid his left arm under Elroy's shoulders. He grabbed a pillow in his right and shoved it under him, moving him into a halfway sitting position. Then he snagged another pillow, bunched it sideway, and used it to prop Elroy's head a bit higher.

Once done, Dermot eased back in his chair.

Elroy lifted the bowl of bone broth and took a tentative sip. His eyebrows shot up. He hummed and took a deeper drink.

"This is good," Elroy murmured. "What is it?"

"Curry flavored bone broth," Dermot told him. "Tasty and nutrient-dense. Great for giving you the strength to heal."

Cocking his head, he quickly added, "You're not a vegetarian or something, are you?"

Snickering, Elroy shook his head. "Naw. Not even close."

"Good." Dermot would have catered to Elroy's needs, but it was nice to know he wouldn't have to. "So…shifters, mates, claiming, and bonding."

Elroy nodded, then went back to his beverage.

"Shifters have increased healing, are stronger, faster, and hardier than humans." Seeing Elroy's eyebrows lift, Dermot was swift to add, "I'm not saying we're better than humans. There's just some differences between us other than our ability to turn into an animal." To his relief, Elroy just smirked, so he continued. "Due to that, shifters can live upwards of five hundred years."

Elroy choked, then began coughing.

"Shit!" Dermot cried, reaching for Elroy. He rubbed his upper back with his right hand, doing his best to soothe him. "I'm so sorry, baby. I should have waited until you'd swallowed." At the same time, he gripped the bowl, making certain it didn't spill all over the place. "I'll be more careful from now on."

Once Elroy stopped coughing, he groaned, the sound full of pain. "Fuck," he whimpered while panting harshly. "Hurts."

Damn it! My thoughtlessness caused my mate to jostle his leg.

Leaning closer, Dermot massaged Elroy's neck as he nuzzled his beard against his temple. He remembered how much his mate had enjoyed that before. All the while, he whispered words of apology.

"I'm okay," Elroy muttered thickly. He sighed deeply and relaxed into the pillows. "I'm okay." Then Elroy turned his head so Dermot's next peck landed on his lips. "Really."

Dermot let out a soft sigh as he took a few seconds to sip at Elroy's plump lips. Reveling in the knowledge that his mate had initiated contact, he savored the moment. Knowing he needed to finish explaining, he eased away.

The sight of Elroy's kiss-swollen lips almost had him diving back in again. He certainly couldn't convince himself to move much further away. Still, he released the bowl and Elroy's nape and rested his forearms on the bed.

Elroy cleared his throat. "So. Five hundred years," he murmured. "That's a long time." Then he took another gulp of his drink.

Once certain Elroy had swallowed, Dermot replied, "That's why Fate gives us a mate. Someone special we can bond with. Their life will extend to match ours, assuming they're human, and the shifter spends the rest of his days caring for, protecting, and pleasing that person." He hesitated an instant, then added, "After I claim you, which involves sex and a claiming bite" — he waggled his eyebrows as he told him — "which will make you orgasm" — he sobered — "we will share a soul bond. There is no divorce, and I'll need you home every night."

Elroy's eyes narrowed. "Bonding is marriage without the hope of divorce?"

Dermot nodded once.

"And how does your Fate decide on who would be right for you?"

Pleased Elroy was asking questions instead of rejecting him out of hand, Dermot shrugged. "That remains unclear. A subject many paranormals have pondered," he admitted. When he spotted Elroy's eyes narrowing, Dermot gently gripped his forearm. "Remember you telling me you were admiring me across the courthouse?"

Dermot still couldn't believe he'd missed this man.

A muscle in Elroy's jaw flexed, but he nodded.

"We were already compatible. Fate just ramps up the desire a little." Dermot rubbed along the soft skin of Elroy's inner arm. "A relationship between a shifter and his mate is still work, but I'll never stray, and my whole world will be devoted to your happiness." Dermot swallowed hard, then admitted, "Just about every paranormal dreams of the day they meet their mate, Elroy, and I'll work very hard to make this adjustment worth your while."

CHAPTER FIVE

Drawing in a deep breath, Elroy took in Dermot's expression...so full of hope.

Elroy had wanted to snag this man's attention the second he'd spotted him walking down the courthouse hallway. Freezing in the doorway, he'd just managed to keep his jaw from sagging open. Richmond had needed to call his name twice to get his attention, so he would finish walking into the conference room. Richmond had let him know in private later.

After a few discreet inquiries, Elroy had learned the piercing-clad lawyer who drove the *Harley* was Rueben Calhoun. Their paths had never directly crossed, but he had certainly dreamed about it. Kyle had noticed and blamed him for cheating on him...which was why his ex had cheated on Elroy, instead.

But do I want him because of Fate?

Oh, who gives a shit why Rueben — Dermot...wants me. He just does.

Stumbling over Dermot's name in his mind, Elroy realized he was missing a few key pieces of information. Between lust and meds, his brain was well and truly scrambled. He downed the last several swallows of the delicious bone broth as he thought about how to phrase his questions.

God, please don't let this be a delusion, and if it is, I don't wanna wake up.

Except, no way do I have a good enough imagination to dream this up.

"So—" Elroy handed the bowl to Dermot, who set it back on the nightstand. "Why did you fake your death? And why are you living out here?"

Dermot's eyebrows shot up.

Obviously, that hadn't been what the man had thought Elroy would ask.

Rubbing the back of his neck, Dermot told him, "Since shifters live so long, every once in a while, we have to take a step back from the human world. Otherwise, friends or acquaintances will notice we don't age as they do." He grimaced before continuing, "Because as my life as Rueben I was a lawyer for my pack, I had a pretty high profile. I worked law for nearly twenty years, and people were beginning to comment on my looks. My persona as Rueben had to come to an end." Lifting his hands, Dermot shrugged his shoulders. "Therefore, a fake death, and me out here in the mountains, away from humans who may recognize me."

Nodding, Elroy understood.

Except—

"That means we can't be seen together. Doesn't it?" Elroy's chest tightened at the thought. "I'll never get to admit to my friends that I have a boyfriend."

Dermot bowed his head and scowled at the mattress. "I'm not certain that's the case," he began slowly. "Did you ever show them a picture of me?"

Elroy wondered at his tone and question for only an instant. Then it clicked. The man was clearly working through possibilities to give him what he wanted...to make him happy.

"Uhhh..." *Did I?* Grimacing, Elroy admitted, "I honestly can't remember. When I first spotted you, about two and a half months before your *death*"—he made air quotes—"I was in a relationship."

"And that would explain why Fate didn't have me cross your path sooner," Dermot commented with a wry smile. "I would have pursued you anyway, and I was already prepping for my *death*." He winked and made air quotes, too. "It would have created a bit of chaos in your life."

"And this timing is any better?" Elroy didn't see it.

Dermot chuckled. "Absolutely. I won't be a homewrecker. You won't feel guilty." He gave Elroy a heated grin. "How about this. We'll give me meeting your friends a try in a secluded environment. If they recognize me, I can have a vampire wipe the encounter from their mind."

Gasping, Elroy tensed…which sent a shard of pain through his leg. He hissed and forced himself to relax.

"You okay?" Dermot swept his gaze over him as he grabbed his hand and massaged his palm. "What happened?"

Elroy scowled at him. "You just dropped the vampire bombshell without a second thought."

For a second, a grimace twisted Dermot's features. "I'm sorry, baby." He brought Elroy's hand to his lips and kissed his knuckles. "I didn't think."

"I'm guessing there are still many things you need to explain."

Dermot nodded, worry filling his brown eyes.

Realizing that accepting Dermot, accepting a life with him, Elroy would be joining a whole new world, he tried to decide if he wanted that.

Is this one man worth turning my life upside down?

Then Elroy met Dermot's deep, earnest gaze. The man—shifter—hid nothing from him. He was open and honest, displaying his desire and hope, his worry and fear, even the concern and tension. Unable to hold Dermot's gaze as his mind whirled, Elroy glanced down…and remembered the man was naked.

And he's still hard as nails.

Elroy's mouth watered with the desire to suck Dermot's massive pierced rod. He wanted to slip his tongue beneath the hoop in his glans and tug lightly. His fingers twitched with the need to rub those balls and discover what they felt like.

Would they —

"Oh, gods, baby. Please, stop lookin' at me like that," Dermot rasped, snapping Elroy's attention to the pained look on his face. "Or let me touch you, please you. Or touch me, or —
"

"Yes," Elroy hissed, interrupting him.

Dermot's eyes widened. He swept his tongue out and whetted his lips, then swallowed so hard his Adam's apple bobbed. "Yes?" His voice had deepened, turning gruff.

The sound of it sent a shock of lust to Elroy's balls, and he realized he was once again hard as nails.

Oh, yeah. I don't mind a little shake-up to my life to experience what Dermot is offering.

"Yes, let's do this. Let's figure this out," Elroy continued, unable to help how breathy he sounded as his excitement mounted. "I know it won't be all roses. It won't be easy, but I've wanted you for so fucking long, and when I thought you'd died —" Elroy paused and swallowed hard.

Elroy had never admitted it to anyone, but his heart had ached. In the privacy of his shower, he'd cried. Although Elroy hadn't understood it at the time, he did now.

This man is the other half of my soul.

"Oh, baby," Dermot murmured roughly. "That will never happen again." Reaching into the nightstand, he pulled out a tube of lube and tossed it on the bed. His dark eyes glimmered with lust as he raked his gaze over Elroy's blanket-covered body. "You're mine, and I'm yours, my mate. Soon, we will be one."

Then Dermot gripped the blanket and carefully pulled it off him.

Elroy noticed the red briefs he wore...and they were not ones he recognized. Snapping his attention back to Dermot, he lifted his eyebrows in silent question. He couldn't quite help the way his mouth opened and closed, no sound escaping him.

Dermot chuckled huskily, his brown eyes twinkling. "I admit I have already seen every inch of you, baby." He placed the rucked up blanket on the boot box at the end of the bed. Returning his focus to Elroy's face, Dermot told him, "I'm the one who found you, soaked and injured. I carried you here and removed your wet clothes."

Clearing his throat, Elroy murmured, "I'm grateful you did."

"Me, too." Dermot roved his gaze over Elroy, a thoughtful look stealing over his features.

"What is it?"

Elroy barely resisted the urge to cover himself. He knew his body was strong and toned from working out at his home gym. While Elroy didn't think he held a candle to Dermot, he'd had enough people compliment him that he felt pretty comfortable in his own skin.

Dermot smiled at him. "Admiring what's mine while trying to figure out the best way to do this so we don't cause you undue pain."

Right. A broken leg.

Glancing around the bed, Elroy nibbled his bottom lip for a second. "I have no idea how I'd get the underwear off," he admitted. He grimaced as he returned Dermot's look. "As much as I don't want to wait, I'm just not sure."

It had only been two days since he'd busted up his leg, after all.

"The way I mentioned earlier is still the best, I think," Dermot replied, smiling hungrily at him. "However, if you end up in pain, let me know, and I'll stop, and I'll give you some more pain meds."

Elroy groaned. "I hate meds."

"Me, too."

Then Dermot picked up a pair of sheers and opened and

closed them, making a *whick, whick* noise. "And your under-wear is easily dealt with."

When Dermot lifted the waistband of Elroy's underwear and slid one of the tines under it, he sucked in a surprised gasp. He let the breath out on a low laugh as he watched his soon-to-be lover cut off his underwear. Elroy thought his erec-tion should have wilted with the proximity of those blades near it, but he didn't soften one iota.

Instead, Elroy felt himself pulse a bead of pre-cum.

Dermot's nostrils flared, and he let out a low moan. "Gods, you smell so good. Can't wait to taste you."

"Y-You can smell me?" Elroy's heart thudded in his chest as Dermot peeled back the destroyed fabric, revealing his bobbing prick. "Oh!"

"Mmm-hmmm," Dermot confirmed right before leaning close and pressing his nose to Elroy's groin. He inhaled nois-ily, displaying no shame in his desires. "Sooooo goooood." His voice came out husky, with an almost drunken quality to it. Then Dermot straightened, revealing a feral smile. "Want to taste your cum, but I'm going to wait."

"Wh-Why?"

Just the idea of Dermot sucking his cock caused his dick to twitch. His heart raced in his chest, and he could barely get moisture into his throat. He wanted to feel Dermot's full lips wrapped around him in the worst way, and he tensed, fighting the urge to thrust.

A stab of pain shot up his leg, drawing a hiss from his lips.

"That's why," Dermot replied. "I need you relaxed and boneless, so I'm going to roll you to your side, slot up behind you, and fondle your prostate." His dark eyes glittered as he narrowed them. "*You* are going to lie there, relax, and accept the pleasure I give you."

Moaning at that visual, Elroy nodded his head eagerly.

Dermot swept his gaze over him again as he set the scissors

aside. Then he rearranged the pillows, leaving one under Elroy's head. He placed the second near Elroy's right hip.

"Take slow, deep breaths, baby," Dermot urged as he gripped Elroy's left hip. "I'm going to lift your leg and move it onto that pillow. This is probably going to hurt," he warned, his voice sounding pinched. "But I'll soothe it with a prostate massage."

Just the idea of moving his leg caused sweat to pop out on Elroy's skin. Still, he wanted this. He wanted everything.

Elroy sprawled his right hand out to the side, so it was out of the way. Then he placed his left palm flat against the mattress, ready to help push. Meeting Dermot's gaze, he nodded.

Dermot gripped his cast at the ankle, then picked up his hip.

Clamping his teeth over his bottom lip, Elroy barely managed to bite back his groan as white-hot agony shot up his leg. Goose bumps broke out all over his body. His skin flushed hot, then cold, and he was nearly instantly drenched in sweat.

"Breathe, baby. Gods, I'm so sorry, Elroy. Breathe, my mate. Shoulda goddamned waited. Gonna make it better."

Elroy heard Dermot's words through the haze of pain that was blanketing him. As much as he wished he could offer reassurance, he knew if he opened his mouth, he would scream. Instead, Elroy focused on breathing and relaxing his body.

The dip of the bed behind him barely registered. The heat at his back warmed him a little, though. When Dermot slid a slick finger into his chute, he almost clenched.

Then, finally, a burst of pleasure cut through the pain. His groin warmed once more. He moaned softly as his prostate was manipulated in the most wonderful of ways. After a few minutes, he acknowledged the sucking kisses on his neck and shoulder.

Sighing deeply, Elroy bowed his head, giving Dermot more room.

"There you go, Elroy," Dermot crooned. "So sorry, baby. Just relax and let go." A hand not his own began playing with his hardening dick. "Let your blood fill this beautiful rod, my mate. I wanna see you straining with your desire."

Between the finger — *no, fingers* — working over his prostate as well as the wet palm massaging him from root to tip, Elroy wouldn't have been able to stop himself from hardening, even if he'd tried.

And he didn't try.

"D-Dermot," Elroy mumbled, then moaned deeply. "Sssoooo g-good."

Elroy had never heard himself slur his words quite like that, but then again, never had someone put so much effort into creating blissful tingles through so many parts of his body.

"Right here, my mate," Dermot rumbled against his shoulder, tickling the fine hairs there. "Stay still, Elroy. Gonna make you fly."

Goose bumps formed on Elroy's flesh for a whole new reason. The base of his spine prickled. Zings continued to erupt from his prostate through his groin. His balls began to tighten. When Dermot massaged his frenulum while dipping a nail into his slit, he lost himself.

Whimpering Dermot's name, Elroy flew. His orgasm roared through his body, blocking out any vestiges of pain. He dug his fingernails into the wrist of the hand on his cock, fearing if he let go, he would float away.

"So beautiful in your passion." Dermot nipped Elroy's shoulder where it met his neck. "Can't wait to see you wear my mark, right here." He did it again. "Gonna fuck you to another orgasm first, though."

Elroy opened his mouth, then closed it again, having no idea what to say. He wasn't certain that was possible, but he would love to see the man try.

"Fuck me," Elroy settled on. "Please, fuck me."

"You never need to beg, baby," Dermot told him as he eased his fingers free. "It'll always be my pleasure. Push out."

A second later, Elroy felt something blunt with a bump against his opening. Even before he acknowledged that would be the prince albert, Dermot eased his crown past his guardian muscle. Elroy gasped at the stretch, then moaned when the man lifted his hand from his spent cock and gripped a nipple, giving it a twist, distracting him.

Feeling a deep groan rumble from the torso pressed against his back, Elroy couldn't help but grin. He turned his head as he rubbed his left hand up Dermot's arm. Peering behind him, he looked at his lover. He took in his closed eyes and features twisted in a pleasure-pain expression.

"Fuck me," Elroy repeated, staring. "Now."

Dermot's eyelids snapped open, and he pinned him with a heated look.

"Always."

Then Dermot began to move, his hot hard cock hitting all Elroy's most sensitive places.

CHAPTER SIX

Sliding into his mate's hot, tight, clenching body felt like coming home.

Dermot had always loved fucking, and he'd done it often. Men, women, short, tall, fat, or skinny, he hadn't cared. If they'd been willing and knew the score, Dermot was good. After all, he would never settle down unless it was with his mate.

And now, miraculously, here he is.

With his left hand clamped firmly on Elroy's hip, Dermot rutted steadily. He kept his mate from moving, so he couldn't aggravate his leg. Aiming for his prostate, he sought to offer his injured human maximum pleasure.

Want to hear my mate scream before I flood his ass.

Dermot kept that goal firmly in mind with each move he made. Knowing his cock piercings would drag along his lover's inner tissues, he made slow deep ruts. He worked the skin of Elroy's nape, neck, and shoulder, pulling up marks as he reveled in the way his mate offered his flesh.

"You're so sexy, Elroy," Dermot murmured huskily between nibbles. "Your body feels exquisite wrapped around my cock." He sucked hard, then whispered, "Soon, I will suck your balls and rim your hole. I'm gonna give you all the pleasure you can possibly stand."

When Dermot began proclaiming all the things he wanted to do to his mate, it had the desired response. Moans and whimpers poured from Elroy's mouth. His chute clutched at Dermot's dick spastically. Even Elroy's body trembled against his own.

It also caused Dermot's own balls to begin tightening dangerously.

"I want to fill you," Dermot claimed, slowing his thrusts, trying to get himself under control. "Will you come on my cock, baby?" He pushed all the way in and paused, pressing his piercings against Elroy's gland. "Wanna feel you squeeze me like you did my fingers."

Dermot began making micro-thrusts. His movements barely gave him stimulation. It wasn't for him, however. He knew it would cause ecstasy-inducing sparks against Elroy's prostate.

"D-Dermot," Elroy whimpered. "O-Oh, oh, oh, there. Oh!"

Grinning at that response, Dermot wrapped his teeth around the flesh where Elroy's neck met his shoulder. He felt his gums tingle, but he fought back the need to allow his canines to descend. Sliding the arm he had under Elroy, Dermot moved it from his mate's nipples back to his groin.

Wrapping his fingers around Elroy's erection, Dermot began sliding his palm from root to tip and back again. He paused at the base to fondle his man's balls. All the while, he continued his tiniest of ruts.

To Dermot's relief, it didn't take long.

Elroy let out an unintelligible wail as he came again, his cock pulsing in Dermot's fist.

Dermot moaned his own relief upon feeling Elroy's inner muscles massage him. With his mate satisfied, he no longer held back his own needs. His balls pulled tight so fast it made his head spin. Then Dermot was pouring his essence into his mate, the other half of his soul.

As Dermot's hips jerked spastically, his dick coating Elroy's inner walls, his canines exploded from his gums. They sank deep into his mate's flesh. A burst of iron-rich fluid poured across his taste buds, and his cock twitched, expelling one last burst of seed.

Drinking greedily, Dermot sucked again and again. Elroy whined and trembled in his hold. He would have felt concern, except then his mate's half-softened penis twitched in his grip, and more seed poured over his fingers.

Hell, yeah. Such an amazing response.

Other shifters hadn't been whistling Dixie when they told him that mates got off on their bites.

Good.

After carefully easing his teeth free of Elroy's flesh, Dermot licked away all traces of his mate's delicious blood. Once certain he'd sealed the wound, he kissed his mark, then relaxed. Gently, he began caressing every bit of skin he could reach.

When that didn't elicit a response, Dermot listened to the steady rhythm of Elroy's breathing. He grinned, smug satisfaction flooding him. He'd given his human so much pleasure that he'd passed out.

Perfect.

Dermot knew that sleep really was the best thing for his injured mate right then. Plus, he'd gotten more pain meds as well as good nutrients into him. That, along with bonding with him, would go a long way in making his mate well again as swiftly as possible.

For several long moments, Dermot floated in the afterglow. He loved having his mate in his arms and his dick in his ass, even soft. Dermot imagined many a night just like this one—without his mate injured.

Finally, however, Dermot forced himself away from Elroy. He carefully eased his prick free and slipped from the bed. Pausing, he stared at the gorgeous specimen of maleness Fate had bestowed upon him.

Elroy sported a lean, strong runner's build. His abdominals were toned, and he had defined muscle definition on his limbs. He kept his black hair cropped short, and from experience, Dermot knew it felt slightly coarse. The man's beautiful medium-brown skin was the exact opposite—smooth and soft.

Gods, and his firm ass cheeks. Damn.

Dermot's fingers twitched just looking at them. Spotting his white seed marking those cheeks made his blood heat and his dick thicken. He could so easily give himself a few strokes, harden back up, and sink right back in there.

Groaning under his breath, Dermot turned away from the sight. He padded naked out of his bedroom and into his bathroom. After wiping himself down, he took fresh towels back to his mate.

Once he was done cleaning Elroy's backside, Dermot hesitated. He worried returning his human to his original position would wake him from the pain. Deciding against it, he carefully pressed the pillow aside enough to clean his mate's front. Then he tucked a clean, dry towel between Elroy and the wet spot. Ever-so-carefully, Dermot tucked the quilt around his mate, keeping it away from his mate's casted leg because he worried it would be too heavy and cause discomfort.

Finally, Dermot picked up the dishes and took them to the kitchen. He left them in the sink in favor of grabbing his cell phone. Grinning, he couldn't hold off sharing his good fortune with his alpha.

Dermot dialed while grabbing a bottle of beer from his fridge.

"Hi, Dermot," Alpha Declan greeted. "How's yer mate?"

Grinning widely, Dermot proclaimed, "Elroy woke up. We've bonded."

As Dermot tucked his phone between his ear and shoulder, then twisted off the cap on the bottle, only to grab his phone in hand again, he heard a long, pregnant pause. If he hadn't been able to hear Declan breathing on the other end of the line, he would have thought it dropped. Unease slithered through him.

51

"Alpha?" Dermot winced, hating how timid his voice sounded.

"I'm sorry, Dermot," his alpha murmured. "I'm, uh —" His quiet chuckle came through the line. "I guess ye could say ye shocked the shit outta me. Congratulations."

Relief flooding him, Dermot felt his unease melt away. "Thank you." He crossed to the living room. After setting his beer down on the side table, he moved toward the fireplace. "I admit, I think it's because the mate-pull has been working on him for around a year." As Dermot threw a log on the fire, he commented, "I still can't believe I missed him all those months ago."

"Gods, a year?" Declan sounded incredulous. "How did ye not know? What does he do there? Somethin' in the background where ye'd never see him?" A popping sound came through the line, as if he'd snapped his fingers. "He's in security and saw ye through monitors?"

Dermot's mind went blank.

"You know, now that you mention it, we never got that far." Picking up his beer, Dermot settled on the sofa. "I have no clue what he does."

"He's a paralegal," another voice said, which Dermot recognized as Beta Dixon Holsteen. "Most likely, you'd never see him in court, but he'd be there on occasion when his boss was meeting a client." The beta made a rude noise. "And, man, that guy is a piece of work. Self-righteous asshole."

For an instant, Dermot bristled, thinking Beta Dixon was talking about Elroy.

"What do ye mean, Dixon?" Alpha Declan questioned. "What's up with Richmond? That's Elroy's boss, by the way, Dermot."

Understanding dawned, and Dermot relaxed. He took a swig of his beer as he listened to Dixon clue them both in.

"Just your typical run-of-the-mill lawyer that values

money over scruples. He has more than a few disreputables as clients." Dixon growled low in his throat. "Elroy's co-worker Lane isn't much better. I'd be happy to meet either one of 'em in a dark alley and offer them a bit of karma."

"Well, damn, Dixon." Alpha Declan's tone sounded droll. "Never heard ye quite this bitter about the injustice of the world, although I know we've only known each other a couple of years." He chuckled low in his throat. "Is this normal for ye, Beta?"

Beta Dixon let out a throaty sigh. "No, Alpha. Sorry." The sound of hands moving over fabric, maybe the beta rubbing his palms over his jeans, came over the line. "Just pissed that the last lead we had on Larson didn't pan out. I hate that the fucker's still on the loose."

"We all do," Alpha Declan stated on a growl. "But we'll get him."

"I hate to say it, but we may need to bring Jared back into the fold." Beta Dixon didn't sound too pleased at the prospect. "His buddy, Raul, is good, but he's not Jared."

Alpha Declan sighed noisily. "I thought you two had worked out yer differences."

"We did," Dixon replied, sounding confused.

"Then ye should know that Jared was never *not* in *our fold*." Dermot heard Alpha Declan stress those last couple of words. "Not to mention, Carson is our pack's head enforcer. They're on vacation."

"Oh." Beta Dixon sounded confused. "I thought they were doing work for your prior beta, recently appointed Council-man Shane Alvaro." He cleared his throat before adding, "Guess I just thought they would be sticking with him."

Laughing softly, Dermot couldn't help but cut in. "There is no way Enforcer Carson would walk away from this pack." As their leading lawyer, he'd been privy to *a lot* of the wolves' inner workings, even if he wasn't considered a member of the inner circle. "Carson's loyalty will always be with Alpha Declan, and Jared's loyalty will always be to Carson. If the alpha calls, they will come."

"Huh, okay." Beta Dixon still sounded confused but for a different reason. "Sorry, Alpha. I guess even after a couple of years, I'm still feeling things out, as the saying goes."

"No problem, Dixon." The loss of formality told Dermot more than Alpha Declan's tone that all had been forgiven. "Anyway, back to you, Dermot. Ye said ye bonded."

"You bonded?" Dixon cut in. "Damn, man. Congrats. How'd he take everything?"

Dermot once again explained that Elroy had been lusting after him for several months prior to his death. Then he shared his thoughts on why Fate had held off on their meeting. Finally, he told of Camilla.

"She's his best friend, and he scented pretty upset at not being able to introduce us. We'll need to use the radio phone so they can chat soon," Dermot told them, then explained his idea. "I'd also like your permission to meet her and Bart. If we have Vince or one of the others nearby, just in case they do actually know my face, we could immediately alter their memories."

"That can be arranged," Declan stated slowly. "I know our desire to please our mate, especially with a newly forged bond, is especially high. Vince and Frankie aren't in the area right now. Freddie is with Reb."

Frankie was a wolf shifter in the pack, and Vince was his vampire mate. Freddie was their young son, and Reb was Frankie's older brother. He and his mate, Daithi, took care of Freddie whenever Frankie and Vince were out of town.

"I know your cover story is that Elroy is with a park ranger," Dermot began slowly, feeling his way. "Is that my identity for the next thirty-plus years?"

"It can be, Dermot. If ye want it to be," Alpha Declan told

him. "Or in a decade when ye return to society, it can be something else. Ye've only been hiding less than a year, and I know Leo hasn't discussed it with ye, yet."

Dermot nodded absently. "True."

"Ye still have time," the alpha assured him. "Ye know, now that ye found yer mate, why don't ye discuss it with him?"

"Huh. That's a good idea," Dermot admitted. "I will."

"And he will keep our secrets?" Beta Dixon pressed.

Even as Dermot nodded, he claimed, "I'll make certain he knows the importance of it."

"Good." The beta could sometimes be a man of few words, not that there was anything wrong with that.

"Call again when ye think yer mate will be awake long enough to schedule a chat with his friend," Alpha Declan told him. "We'll get it set up."

"Will do, Alpha."

"And, Dermot."

Dermot waited.

"Congratulations."

Grinning, Dermot replied, "Thank you, Alpha."

The line disconnected, and Dermot turned his attention to his open bedroom door. His mate waited.

Smiling, Dermot rose. He made a quick stop in the restroom to piss and clean up. Then he went to his bedroom, slipped into bed, and cuddled with his mate.

CHAPTER SEVEN

The ache of Elroy's bladder pulled him from the dredges of some of the best sleep of his life. The warmth of a body pressed against his backside as well as the arm around his middle caused his lips to curve into a smile. Turning his head and stretching sent a shaft of pain through Elroy's leg, and he hissed and tensed.

"Easy, Elroy." Dermot's deep sexy, sleep-roughened voice crooned into his ear. At the same time, his arm tightened, keeping him still. "Don't move, yet. We slept the night through." Easing his hold, Dermot lifted onto his elbow and peered down at him with a concerned frown. "Sorry, baby. I shoulda woke you to take some pain relievers, but I forgot to set my alarm."

"Is'okay," Elroy slurred, working through the throbbing discomfort.

Dermot shook his head, most likely reading the pain on his face. "It's really not." He pecked a kiss to his lips, then began to draw away.

"Wait." Elroy lifted his good hand.

Clasping Elroy's palm with his own, Dermot squeezed lightly. "I'll be right back. I have a glass of water and the meds on the dresser." He pointed. "Remember?"

Elroy did remember, but that wasn't the issue. "I need to pee." His bladder twinged again. "Now."

Dermot's brows shot up, then down again as he nodded. "Right. Uh." He glanced from Elroy's blanket-covered groin, to the dresser, then back to his face. "We can do this two ways.

I can carry you to the bathroom, which is gonna really hurt." Dermot grimaced, obviously not liking that idea. "Or I can get a bottle and help you pee in it so you don't have to leave the bed."

Okay. Maybe it's the second option he doesn't like.

"Your choice."

Groaning, Elroy realized he didn't like either option, either. "Give me a pain pill, then carry me to the bathroom."

No way do I want his help peeing in a bottle.

Grimacing again, Dermot released Elroy's hand and slid from the bed.

Upon seeing Dermot's flexing, naked ass as he moved to the dresser, Elroy nearly swallowed his tongue.

Just damn! I bet I could bounce a quarter off those firm globes.

Even Elroy's dick began to swell.

Shit!

Elroy turned his head away from the enticing sight and focused on the pulsing in his leg. That caused any hope for an erection to die a swift death. Breathing slowly, he waited.

Fortunately, not for long.

"Here, Elroy," Dermot stated, the bed dipping beside Elroy. "Let me help you sit up a smidge. I didn't know if you wanted half again or all of it since you're about to be in agony."

Seeing a pill broken in two pieces cradled on Dermot's palm, Elroy quickly debated. "Just half to start." He met his lover's concerned gaze. "I really am a lightweight, and I hate how I feel on meds."

"I can respect that," Dermot replied. "Take the water."

Elroy obeyed.

Dermot placed half the pill on the nightstand. Then he tipped the other into Elroy's mouth while sliding his free hand under his shoulders. He lifted a little, making it easy for Elroy to take a swallow of water.

His bladder ached.

Quickly holding out the water, Elroy murmured, "Let's do this."

Nodding, Dermot took the glass and set it aside. "Relax as best as you can."

Elroy opened his mouth, then squeaked.

Dermot had slid his second arm under his thighs and lifted him into his arms.

As soon as Elroy's left leg swing from the pillow, a spike of pain speared up it. He hissed and bowed his head. His cast bumped into Dermot's side, and he groaned through gritted teeth. Black spots danced across his vision, and he breathed noisily, fighting them back.

"Shit, baby. I'm so sorry," Dermot murmured, his tone full of self-deprecation. "So stupid of me. I should have picked you up from the other side. Goddamnit!"

"S'okay," Elroy tried to say, but he wasn't certain Dermot could even understand him.

"Almost there," Dermot encouraged. "Two more steps." Then he asked, "Can you put the seat down?"

Through hazy vision, Elroy saw they'd made it to the bathroom, and Dermot was crouching beside the toilet. He lifted a trembling hand. Shock filled him at how rung out he felt just from that short trip.

"Never mind," Dermot countered. "I can do it."

Dermot straightened, leaned against the counter, and lifted his right leg. Using that knee, he knocked the toilet seat down. Then he carefully deposited Elroy upon it.

Groaning, Elroy didn't even wait until Dermot had left. He released the clench he'd had on his bladder and let go. Even with the pain coursing up his leg, he still sighed with relief.

When the damp towel swiped across Elroy's forehead, he almost jolted off the toilet.

Dermot's hand on his shoulder steadied him, and Elroy felt the cloth again. "Easy, baby," his lover murmured. "You're okay. You'll be okay."

Elroy peeled open eyelids he hadn't even realized he'd closed. "I'm still peeing," he whispered, because he was, and he felt more than a little uncomfortable.

"And I'm taking care of my mate," Dermot countered, massaging his shoulder with one hand while wiping the sweat from Elroy's brow with the cloth. "That took a lot more out of you than we thought it would."

Closing his eyes again, Elroy sighed deeply. His urine stream dwindled and stopped. He relaxed, realizing it was a damn intimate moment with his lover.

God, I have a lover again. One who will never leave me.

Elroy smiled.

"Feeling better?" Dermot asked softly.

"Yeah," Elroy whispered back, not wanting to break the moment. Except, then his stomach grumbled.

Dermot chuckled. "Sounds like I should feed you."

Peering up at Dermot, Elroy asked, "Mind if I brush my teeth first?" He furrowed his brows as he added, "Maybe I'll just sit here until the painkiller kicks in."

Nodding, Dermot agreed. "That's a good idea. I'll start breakfast. When you're ready to brush your teeth, I'll give you a bowl of water and a toothbrush."

"You have spares up here?" For some reason, Elroy found that…surprising.

Dermot shook his head. "Nope. When Alpha Declan shared the news with my pack's inner circle that I'd found my mate and he was here and injured, they picked up some necessities for you and brought them out."

"Huh. Nice of them."

Leaning down, Dermot pecked a too-short, too-soft kiss to Elroy's lips before telling him, "We take care of our own." Then he kissed him again, licking and nipping at his lips and tongue. "Just relax a minute and call me when you're ready."

Elroy nodded.

Dermot left.

For a few minutes, Elroy just sat and let his mind drift. He thought about how his life had changed. He wondered why he'd accepted everything — and Dermot — so swiftly.

Elroy had never believed in love at first sight, but that was what this had felt like. He'd had a head-over-heels crush on Dermot the second he'd seen him in the courthouse hall. That had been almost three months before Dermot had faked his death eight months ago. Learning of his death had gutted him, even though he'd never met him.

Then Kyle had accused Elroy of cheating with the man. While he'd denied it, which was the truth, he still hadn't been able to stop himself from mourning the man. So Kyle hadn't believed him, had stepped out himself, and they'd broken up.

Until the prior evening, Elroy hadn't been with anyone else.

Was I unconsciously saving myself for my soulmate who was alive and waiting?

Elroy had never believed in such things before, but now that he knew paranormals existed, maybe Fate and divine destiny were real, too.

Realizing his head was beginning to spin with his thoughts, Elroy blinked and cleared his vision.

Pain meds kicked in.

Sighing, Elroy shook his head. At least they were doing their job. The stabbing pain in his leg had simmered to a dull ache. *That* he could tolerate.

"Dermot?" Elroy had intended to holler, but his voice came out a soft rasp. He swallowed, planning to try again.

Dermot appeared. "Hey, baby. You feeling a little better?"

Elroy nodded, offering his wolf a wan smile.

My wolf. He does look a little wolfish with his shaggy hair, beard, and intense eyes.

He giggled.

Oh, shit.

Shaking his head, Dermot crouched before him. "Sorry, Elroy. You're definitely right. You are a lightweight." Skimming his blunt fingertips along Elroy's jaw, he winked. "And I *am* your wolf."

"Oh, god. Where's a hole when you need one," Elroy grumbled, mortified that he'd said that out loud.

"No holes, baby." Dermot pecked a kiss to his forehead and straightened. "Let's get you washed up a little, then some food in you, and you'll feel ten times better."

Elroy hoped Dermot was right.

Lying on the sofa instead of the bed, Elroy sighed contentedly. He had a belly full of bacon, eggs, and hash browns, his casted leg was propped up on the far arm of the sofa, and his head was on Dermot's thigh. Even better than listening to the fire crackling was the feel of his lover teasing his fingertips along his neck and shoulders.

"Ready to see if Camilla is available?" Dermot asked.

"Mmmm," Elroy hummed, tipping his head to meet Dermot's gaze. "Almost dozed off."

Dermot grinned. "You can doze off after your call."

Elroy nodded. "Good idea. I know my friends must be worried out of their minds."

"Remember, no mentioning shifters, Rueben, or paranormals," Dermot stated as he reached toward the side table. "I'm Ranger Dermot Reever, and we're trapped in this cabin for another day as my co-workers clear the landslide that wiped out the road." Setting down a device that looked like a radio with a walkie-talkie attached to it, Dermot winked. "And you and I are falling madly in love while I'm taking care of you."

Nodding again, Elroy snorted. "She's going to question that, saying I just have Florence Nightingale effect and should take some time away from you to see if it's real."

A low growl rumbled from Dermot's chest, and he scowled at him. "That's *not* what's happening here." His hand on Elroy's throat wrapped around it and urged his chin up a little. "We are fated mates, and we will build a life together. You're it for me, Elroy Greer."

Warmth bubbled in Elroy's chest as he stared at Dermot's intense expression. "I know." He squeezed his lover's wrist with his left hand, trying to soothe him. "You're my shifter, and I'm your human. Mated and bonded for life."

Dermot let out a long breath between pursed lips, his expression softening. "Yeah." His hand loosened, and he teased his fingertips along Elroy's pulse point. "Sorry. Did I mention shifters are possessive of their mates?" His lips curved into a sheepish smile. "The idea of someone trying to get between us, for any reason—" Dermot shrugged.

"It's fine. I, uh…found it hot," Elroy admitted, glancing pointedly at his dick, which tented his sweat shorts.

Groaning, Dermot muttered, "Gods, baby. I can't do anything about that right now, and—"

The crackling of the radio phone that Dermot had placed on the sofa near Elroy's hip interrupted him. A deep garbled voice came through the speaker. Dermot reached over and fiddled with the knobs, and the reception cleared.

"This is Ranger Holsteen," the man said. "Ranger Reever, can you read me? Over."

Elroy knew from Dermot's explanations over breakfast about the pack and their inner circle that this was Dixon Holsteen, the beta.

Dermot picked up the microphone and pushed a button. "This is Ranger Reever. I read you, Dixon. I have Elroy here beside me. Over."

"How is Elroy holding up, Dermot?" Dixon asked. "And I have Camilla and Bart here with me. They've been worried about him. Over."

"I'll let Elroy speak for himself. Hang on."

Then Dermot handed the microphone to Elroy.

"Hi, Camilla. Bart. I'm sorry to have worried you," Elroy began. "I got turned around in a rainstorm and fell down an embankment." He figured it would be better to downplay it, since cliff sounded so deadly...even though it could have been. "Dermot, uh, Ranger Reever found me and took me to safety." At Dermot's soft reminder, Elroy added, "Over."

Camilla's voice came over the line. "You total asshole. You scared ten years off my life."

Elroy easily heard the fear mixed with relief in Camilla's voice. He opened his mouth, intending to apologize, but Dermot whispered, "She didn't say over. Wait."

While Elroy nodded, Camilla continued, "Just wait until you get back here. I'm gonna paddle your ass." After a heartbeat, where Elroy heard Dermot growl and he patted his lover's leg awkwardly with his bandaged right hand, Camilla said in a more subdued voice, "I heard you were injured. Is it bad?" After a few seconds, she added, "Over."

While Elroy's initial instinct was to tell her, "I'm fine," and gloss over it, he knew he couldn't. Hell, he was sporting a big-ass cast. "Well, I'll be on crutches for a few weeks," he told her glancing at Dermot for guidance, but he just smiled encouragingly. "I broke my leg." Elroy knew his healing would speed up, so while typical recovery time would have been a lot longer, he claimed, "It was a clean break though, and Dermot had a doctor on the line who walked him through bandaging me up. He's taking real good care of me. Over."

"God, man." That was Bart. "If I hadn't flaked, none of this would have happened. I'm so damn sorry. Over."

"To be honest, Bart. I'm glad you did," Elroy stated, needing to reassure his friend. "If this hadn't happened, I wouldn't have met Dermot, and—" He nibbled his bottom lip, struggling with how to explain.

Camilla didn't wait for him to say, "Over."

"Are you seriously telling me that you and Ranger Reever are getting it on while holed up in that little ranger cabin?" Camilla cackled into the line. "Oh my god! You little minx. Finally getting over that asshat, who—"

"Sorry, Elroy." It seemed Bart had snatched the microphone from her. "Uh, you, too, Dermot. So, it sounds like we both found some silver linings to all this. Over."

Elroy's brows shot up. "Oh? What's yours, Bart?" Then he grinned. "Did you finally get your head out of your ass and ask Camilla out? Over."

"Well, I may have done more than just ask her out," Bart admitted. "We'll have to double date. When do you think they'll have you out of there? Over."

"I have no idea," Elroy admitted, not really in any hurry to leave Dermot's love nest, especially since his lover couldn't go to the city with him. "You'll have to ask Ranger Holsteen. Over."

"There is one more thing we have to share with you." Camilla had taken the microphone back. "It's, uh…well, your apartment was broken into. First your car, then your apartment?" A new thread of tension crept into Camilla's voice. "What's going on, Elroy? Who did you piss off? Over."

"My apartment?" Elroy whispered. He felt Dermot's leg tense under his head, and his grip on his shoulder tightened. "When? Over."

"Sometime between Saturday when you went hiking and Sunday when I went looking for you at your place," Camilla told him. "At first, I thought you'd been kidnapped. I called the police and Bart, and he told me about you hiking alone." Her words picked up speed, betraying her rising panic. "Then the cops found your car at the trailhead, and we started search parties, but we were immediately contacted by Ranger McIntire, and he explained where you were. God, Elroy. What the hell is going on with your life?"

Elroy wished he knew.

CHAPTER EIGHT

Seeing his mate's vacant expression and scenting his unease, Dermot took the microphone from his loose grip. He rubbed over his claiming mark to soothe Elroy as he spoke into the device. "I'm afraid Elroy is in a bit of shock, Camilla. Thank you for telling us." Dermot hesitated an instant, then decided to offer, "I'm not much on the city, and I can't get away from Stone Ridge for a while, but if you and Bart want to come up here for a barbeque with me, Elroy, and a few ranger buddies, I'd sure be happy to meet the two most important people in my man's life. Over."

Dermot knew his alpha would happily host them.

"Thanks for the invite," Bart answered. "We'll set something up. Over."

"Since Elroy's injured and his apartment was broken into, I'm not comfortable with him returning there." Dermot sure hoped Elroy wasn't going to fight him on this, but if he did, he knew he could make his mate see reason. "I'm gonna keep him at my cabin up here until the police figure out who's targeting him. Over."

Even if Elroy's car hadn't been broken into, just his home invasion would have been enough to spike Dermot's protective instincts. As it was, now he understood Fate's timing even better. His mate needed him and the protection of his pack.

"A-Are you sure?" Camilla asked, her concern clear in her tone. "Um, you can come stay with me, Elroy. Over."

Dermot focused on Elroy. "I really want you here, my

66

mate." Rubbing his hand over his human's shoulder, massaging lightly, he added, "My pack will step in and help. Find out what the police know. If you've been targeted twice, we need to figure out who it is and stop them." Seeing the uncertainty on Elroy's face as he nibbled his bottom lip, Dermot added, "I need to know you're safe, baby. Let me take care of you."

"What about my job?"

That's not a no.

Grinning, Dermot winked. "With that injury, it'd be a perfect time to quit. There are law offices closer that the pack could get you on at when the time comes."

Elroy's eyes widened. "You're actually asking me to move in with you. Aren't you?"

Dermot cleared his throat, feeling his cheeks heat.

Busted!

Refusing to lie to his mate, Dermot nodded. "Yeah. Shifters do things fast. Especially when bonding with a fated mate."

Groaning, Elroy turned his head and stared into the fire.

Dermot could smell the conflicting scents rising from Elroy — desire, need, concern, disbelief, and even some fear. His mate wanted to give in, but his human mind was having a hard time processing so many changes. Dermot knew it didn't help that he couldn't go out to normal, everyday places with him.

"Elroy." Beta Dixon's voice came through the radio phone. "Whatever you decide, I'll make sure it happens."

Pulling his focus away from the fire, Elroy met Dermot's gaze. His mate knew what Dixon was saying. The beta wouldn't allow Dermot to force him to stay there.

Not that I would do that anyway.

When Elroy held out his hand, Dermot handed the microphone to him. "Thank you, Ranger Holsteen. I appreciate that. Um" — he continued to hold Dermot's gaze as he finished — "I think I'd like to stay with Dermot. At least for now, while I'm healing and the cops figure out what's going on. Over."

Dermot couldn't stop his grin even if he'd wanted to. He didn't even try. "Thank you, baby," he whispered. Bending awkwardly, he pressed his lips to Elroy's in a slow, sipping kiss. Just as he swiped his tongue over his mate's bottom one, asking for entrance, Beta Dixon spoke again.

"We have a couple of detective buddies. I bet one of them can do some digging into your case," the beta claimed. "I'll make some inquiries. Over."

Dermot wanted to thank the beta, but Elroy beat him to it. "Thank you, Ranger Holsteen." Then he winked at Dermot. "From both of us. Over."

Dixon's chuckle came through the line before he offered, "Call me Dixon, man. Titles aren't necessary right now. Oh, Camilla is making *gimme, gimme* gestures."

Elroy snickered, and Dermot grinned.

His mate was staying.

"As soon as that landslide is cleared, and Ranger Holsteen said it would be tomorrow, I'm coming to check on you, Elroy Greer. Do you hear me? Oh, and why haven't you been answering your phone? Your boss called me because I'm your emergency contact. Boy was he pissed." She actually growled through the line. "Once I told him what happened, he still wasn't very nice. How do you work for that jerk? Over."

"Well, I won't be working for him much longer," Elroy told her, grinning at Dermot. "There's been some problems there for a while, so I'm going to use this excuse to find something else. And my phone broke when I fell." Smirking at Dermot, Elroy added, "And I look forward to your shit, bestie of mine, and Dermot looks forward to meeting you and Bart. Over."

"He better," Camilla stated haughtily. "Well, I gotta head to work. You get plenty of rest, El. Love you. Over."

"Love you, too, Cam. Over."

Dermot gritted his teeth, hating listening to Elroy say he

loved someone other than him.

"No more getting into trouble, buddy," Bart ordered, warmth in his tone. "Glad you're okay. See you soon. Over."

"Back atcha, man," Elroy replied. "Over."

"We'll see you tomorrow, guys," Dixon told them. "Over and out."

Dermot turned off the radio phone before picking it up and putting it back on the side table. Returning his attention to Elroy, he waggled his brows. "Whatever shall we do for the next twenty-four hours?"

To Dermot's pleasure, Elroy chuckled. "Are all paranormals horn-dogs?" Then he barked a laugh. "Horn-dog. Dog! Because you're a wolf. Get it?"

Smirking, Dermot shook his head. "That was horrible, my mate." He narrowed his eyes. "But since you're injured, I'll let it pass." Then Dermot sobered. "Paranormals do have a heightened sex drive, but the reason I want to suck you off is because an orgasm is a natural painkiller." Seeing the way Elroy's eyes widened and his brows shot up, he leveled a lascivious smile at him. "And I want to taste your seed and explore your balls before I slide my pierced dick back into you."

Just talking about his desires caused Dermot's cock to flood. His heartrate spiked, and his nostrils flared. When the scent of Elroy's arousal filled the air, his mouth watered.

"Yes, please," Elroy whispered.

Dermot didn't make Elroy repeat himself. Carefully, he lifted his mate's head and slid out from under him. As he stood over his reclining lover, he took in his position on the sofa as well as his injuries.

With a small smile, Dermot met Elroy's gaze. "I was definitely thinking with my dick, and now I realize there's no comfortable way to fuck you on this sofa. Not until you've healed up a bit more." Seeing the disappointment fill Elroy's dark eyes, he quickly added, "However, that doesn't mean

I'm not going to suck your dick."

When Dermot began to kneel and reach for the waistband of Elroy's sweat shorts, his mate gripped his thigh. "No. Not like that."

Cocking his head, Dermot waited. He would do whatever his mate needed to be comfortable.

Elroy patted Dermot's thigh. "Take those off, then swing up here." He licked his lips as his focus drifted to Dermot's groin. "I wanna suck you, too."

Letting out a groan, Dermot nodded. Happy to get on board with that, he gripped the waistband of his sweats and shoved them down, freeing his erection. He immediately returned to the sofa, placing his knees on either side of Elroy's head.

"Oh, look at this beauty," Elroy murmured, immediately wrapping one hand around Dermot's length, sending a spike of awareness to his balls. "Soooo pretty with all this jewelry."

When Elroy used the fingertips of his other hand to flip Dermot's prince albert hoop back and forth, he nearly lost it right then. Only gritting his teeth and recalling his mangled *Harley* pulled him back from the edge. His mate massaging the balls of his jacob's ladder forced Dermot to recall the time he'd gotten his wolf leg stuck in a poacher's snare almost eighty years before.

Shaking his head, Dermot returned his attention to Elroy's erection. The shaft was clearly outlined under the soft fabric, since he hadn't offered his mate underwear. Gripping the waistband, he pulled it up, then down, revealing his long, slender, dark-skinned dick.

Dermot had just tucked the band under Elroy's low-slung balls when his mate wrapped his lips around his crown. Groaning, he trembled, a shiver working up his spine. He swallowed hard and returned his focus to pleasing his lover.

Lowering to his forearm, Dermot opened his mouth as he

gripped the base of Elroy's shaft. He wasted no time in wrapping his lips around his mate's crown. Sucking strongly, he swiped his tongue over his head, scooping up tasty beads of pre-cum and rolling them around his tongue.

To Dermot's smug satisfaction, Elroy paused in his ministrations to his cock. His mate moaned, the vibration on his erection nearly derailing Dermot's concentration, and more pre-cum bubbled from him. Swallowing that, too, he sank further down Elroy's shaft while cradling his mate's balls, gently rolling them, testing his human's sensitivity.

Elroy groaned again, then teased his tongue over the ball embedded in Dermot's frenulum.

It was Dermot's turn to moan roughly. His hips twitched, and he barely resisted the urge to rut. His gut clenched as he fought back his orgasm.

Holy fucking hell! How can I be so close already?

While Dermot knew his piercings made his genitals ultra-sensitive, he'd never experienced sensations like this.

Is it just because he's my mate?

Bobbing on Elroy's cock, Dermot tried to match Elroy's skilled mouth and tongue, but it was no contest. His mate worked his piercings to perfection. His lover's hands massaged his balls, rolling and teasing them. Elroy even managed to deep throat him, repeatedly squeezing around his crown.

Dermot would have felt jealous of whoever Elroy had learned on, but since he was going to be benefiting from his mate's skills for hundreds of years—and Elroy was blowing every thought out of his head—he couldn't.

Then the hand on Dermot's balls skimmed backward.

To Dermot's surprise, Elroy popped off his dick, drawing a whine from him.

Elroy chuckled, the sound husky, low, and oh-so-sexy. "Look at what I just found." Then Elroy took Dermot's dick deep again...as he fondled his guiche piercing.

Unable to help himself, Dermot popped off Elroy's dick

and arched, roaring as he drove his prick deeper into his mate's mouth. Fire shot up his spine as his balls tightened mind-numbingly fast. His body took over as Elroy rolled his guiche over and over, and shards of pleasure-pain burst through Dermot's groin.

Dermot's orgasm slammed through his system, whiting out his vision. Shudders racked his body as he poured his seed down Elroy's throat. The sucking and petting to his cock and balls sent him soaring to heights never before experienced during a blowjob, and he feared he would pass out.

When Dermot's senses began to slowly return, a whimper escaped him. He was resting his head on Elroy's right thigh, but it was what he was feeling below that created delicious aftershocks to ping through his system. Elroy was gently petting his ball sack, and he still had the crown of Dermot's cock in his mouth. His mate suckled him ever-so-lightly, licking over his prince albert, as if he was enjoying a lollipop.

The sensations kept Dermot beyond stimulated, and tremors continued to quake through him.

"M-Mate," Dermot gasped out. He couldn't decide if he wanted to pull away or lay there forever.

Elroy responded by teasing his fingertip over Dermot's hole.

Grunting, Dermot tried to spread his legs wider, nearly falling off the sofa in the process.

Finally, Elroy moved his head, allowing Dermot's crown to slip from his lips. A husky chuckle rumbled through the body beneath him. He petted Dermot's flank and ass.

"God, Dermot," Elroy murmured roughly. "I fucking love your piercings. So, so hot."

Dermot swallowed, trying to get moisture into his too-dry throat. His mate had damn near rung him out with a blowjob. Hell, he was still on edge, his cock semi-hard and his balls tingling.

"I-I…" Dermot found himself at a loss for words.

Elroy sighed deeply, the sound one of smug satisfaction. "The fact that I can unravel a man who has over a hundred years of fucking under his belt" — he hummed — "quite the ego trip. Fuck."

Dermot smiled and offered a rough laugh of his own. "You did, my mate. Gods." Finally, he focused enough to notice Elroy's semi-hard shaft a few inches from his face. White seed coated not only Elroy's stomach and groin but Dermot's chest and stomach as well. "You came."

Chuckling softly, Elroy mumbled, "Hell, yeah, I came. Drinking you, seeing you fall apart. What an aphrodisiac." Elroy rubbed a palm over his ass again. "But you're getting heavy, so I'm gonna ask you to move."

Groaning, Dermot drew together enough coordination to lift onto his arms. He slowly eased off his mate, his limbs trembling. Sliding off the side of the sofa, he rested on his calves with his arms on the cushion.

Leaning forward, Dermot cradled Elroy's head with one hand and took his mate's mouth. He thrust in his tongue and petted his human's interior with slow, languid strokes. Tasting his release on Elroy's tongue, Dermot moaned with pleasure.

Dermot ended the kiss slowly, sucking on Elroy's bottom lip for a moment. Ignoring his once more thickening prick, he stared at his man. He saw the relaxed, satisfied look on Elroy's face, and his heart fluttered in his chest.

"Damn. That is a good look on you," Dermot whispered, teasing his fingertip along Elroy's jaw. "Gonna do my best to put it there often."

Elroy grinned up at him, the expression a little bliss-drunk and sexy as hell. "I look forward to that." Then he winked. "Thanks for the painkillers. I like your kind better than Lark's."

Barking a laugh, Dermot nodded. "Me, too."

They spent the rest of the day sharing food and stories, lounging on the sofa before the fire, making out, and exchanging blowjobs.

Dermot knew he would never get enough of Elroy's mouth, and he knew he would never have to.

CHAPTER NINE

Elroy did his best to tamp down his unease, but from the worried gleam in Dermot's dark eyes, he knew some of it could still be scented.

And isn't that a weird thought. Paranormals can smell emotions...and lies. Wow!

"It'll be okay, Elroy," Dermot assured, reaching over and giving his upper arm a squeeze. "You're pack now. These people will become your new family. They'll always have your back."

Doing his best to offer a reassuring smile, Elroy grabbed Dermot's hand and squeezed. "I do get it. It's just been a bit of a mind-fuck the last couple of days. Ya know?" He tapped his temple with the fingertips of his bandaged hand. "I'll get it all straightened out up here soon enough."

Dermot nodded, squeezing his fingers back. "Understood. In the meantime, I'll stand beside you and comfort you whenever you need it." Winking, he added, "And we do love giving each other comfort."

Elroy chuckled as a burst of arousal caused his blood to simmer. For some reason, even injured and in pain, a provocative look from Dermot would set his blood on fire. His prick would quickly sit up and beg for attention.

"I'm pretty sure I've had more orgasms in the last two days than I have in the past year." Realizing he'd said that out loud, he grimaced. "Should have only taken a quarter of a pill. I'm gonna ask Lark what that shit is."

"I'm sorry it messes with your head a bit, baby," Dermot

replied with compassion. "But since I can't administer orgasmic painkillers at the alpha's house, we had to go this route."

Nodding, Elroy understood. Then Dermot turned his *Jeep* onto a gravel driveway, and he straightened a little in his seat. Peering forward, a surge of anticipation filled him.

Better than uneasiness.

Elroy's lips parted when he caught sight of the house — massive lodge — that appeared through the trees. "Wow." He swept his gaze over the stone fascia that covered the first three feet of the home, then dark wood paneling began. "Your alpha and his mate live *here*?" The home was a sprawling two stories and absolutely gorgeous.

"You could say our pack is quite wealthy," Dermot told him. "Our pack accountant, Rainy MacDougal, is an expert in the stock market. Plus, our pack owns a number of businesses in Stone Ridge and a couple in Sugar Creek."

"Which is why you told me I didn't have to work if I didn't want to," Elroy commented, understanding dawning. Then he smiled wryly at Dermot. "But I would get bored to tears if I sat around all day, every day. I'm just not stagnant like that."

Dermot nodded. "I understand. I have a hard time with it, too, which is why I'm working at a pack-owned lumber business." He parked his *Jeep*, then smirked at him. "Keeps me busy, and I don't have to interact with any humans."

Elroy returned his nod. "Maybe I'll join you there." He'd never worked with his hands, but it sounded interesting. Then he realized how presumptuous that had been, and he felt heat rush to his cheeks. He hoped his dark skin hid it as he rushed to say, "Um, you know…if they need more help."

Lifting their twined fingers to his lips, Dermot kissed his knuckles. "I know what you meant." Then he winked and dropped his hand. "Sit tight. I'll come around."

Watching Dermot round the hood of his vehicle, Elroy rested his hands in his lap. He also noticed the lodge's front door open. Several people poured from the home's depths as

Dermot opened his door. There was quite the mix of people—from black to Caucasian, blond to redhead, huge guys and twinks.

Elroy wrapped his arms around Dermot's neck as his lover slid his hands under him. Suddenly, he didn't feel nearly as nervous. The guys were all smiling at him and Dermot, clearly happy they'd found each other.

Plus, many of them had their arms around each other in pairs, proving the place to be a very gay-friendly home.

While it still hurt for his leg to be dangling that way, Elroy managed to keep from grimacing.

As they approached, the large black man with his arm slung around a small blond wearing make-up stepped backward and indicated the door. "I'm Alpha Declan McIntire. Welcome to me home, Elroy." He grinned, showing off straight white teeth. "And welcome to me pack. It's good to officially meet ye."

Elroy recognized an Irish accent, finding it pleasing to the ear. "Thank you, Alpha. I appreciate everything you and your people have been doing for me."

"Hi, Elroy." The blond stepped forward. "I'm Doctor Lark Trystan." He pointed at a broad-shouldered redhead. "And that's Manon Lemelle. He's a paramedic. We fixed up your leg, and I'd like to check it over again, if that's okay with you. See how the healing is coming since you bonded."

Hearing Lark speak of bonding—which meant sex—so openly and frankly, Elroy felt heat rush to his cheeks once more. "Uh, yeah," he managed to get out. "A-And thank you both for, um, helping me."

"It is our pleasure, *mon ami,*" Manon told him with a grin. "Always happy to help."

Elroy cocked his head, recognizing a Cajun accent.

Huh.

Then Manon kissed the black-haired, androgynous-featured man next to him. "I be down soon, *mon cher.*"

The man just smiled and nodded.

As Dermot carried Elroy upstairs, he heard a cultured-sounding voice he didn't recognize ask, "They have finished their bond, right?"

Dixon's deep voice answered. "Yes."

"And you said he had a deep cut on his right palm and wrist?" the stranger questioned.

"Yes," Dixon replied again. "Why?"

"I'd like to see it."

"Sure. I'll introduce you," Dixon told him, even though technically Elroy hadn't actually been introduced to the beta yet, either — not in person, anyway.

Dermot carried Elroy upstairs and into what was clearly an examination room. His lover placed him on a cloth-covered bed before grabbing a pillow and sliding it under his leg, elevating it. Then Dermot took Elroy's left hand in his own and leaned against the bed.

Plenty of people followed them in.

While Lark pulled out supplies, Alpha Declan made the rest of the introductions.

"This is Beta Dixon Holsteen. I believe ye talked with him on the radio phone?"

Elroy nodded as he met the huge Caucasian's ice-blue eyes. "Good to finally meet you. Thank you for helping my friends. I know they were worried."

Dixon's lips quirked in a half-smile. "Happy to help."

Declan pointed at a lean and toned, dark-haired man. "This is Sebastian Russo. Everyone calls him Seb." Turning to the man, he added, "I appreciate ye coming to give us a hand, seeing as ye're supposed to be here on vacation."

"It is always a pleasure to reinforce ties between shifters and vampires," Sebastian replied with a relaxed smile.

Elroy gasped. "You're a vampire?"

Sebastian nodded once. "I am. Pleased to meet you, Elroy,

and congratulations." He grinned as he shifted his gaze to Dermot. "And to you, too, Dermot."

Dermot nodded. "Thank you." He also squeezed Elroy's hand. "Relax, baby. He's a friend of the pack."

"I-I know." Elroy blew out a breath. "It just, um, startled me." He met Sebastian's gaze and forced a smile. "I'm still getting acclimated."

"Understandable," Sebastian replied, appearing nonplussed. "It's a lot to take in."

"Totally." Elroy snickered, then became aware that Lark was cutting the bandage off his hand. "I'm not sure I want to see this. I'm not real good with blood."

Cradling his jaw, Dermot urged him to look at him. "Then don't look, baby." He smiled warmly as he winked. "Although, I didn't do too bad a job."

"You stitched me up?" Surprise filled Elroy. "I didn't think you were a doctor."

Dermot grinned. "Had one on speed dial, though."

"And you did do a good job," Lark commented. "And it's healing quite nicely. I'm gonna put some salve on it, then rewrap it," the doctor explained to him. "We'll probably have to take the stitches out in only another day or two."

"When you lick your claiming bite, does it heal the skin?" Sebastian asked.

"Aye, it does," Alpha Declan confirmed. "Why?"

"A vampire's saliva does the same to our donors and beloveds," Sebastian replied. "Perhaps, if Dermot bathed the wound in his saliva, it would speed up the healing process even further?"

Declan hummed. "Interesting idea. Did ye want to try it?"

Dermot turned his attention to Elroy. "Do you have a problem with me giving it a go?"

"Uhhhh…it sounds kinda gross to me," Elroy admitted, lifting one shoulder in a shrug. "But it's totally up to you. I'm all for faster healing."

After releasing Elroy's hand, Dermot rounded the bed. He gently cradled his cut palm in his own. Elroy could feel his lover's tongue moving across his flesh, but he didn't look at him. He had no desire to swoon or pass out in front of all these near-strangers.

"Huh. It's working," Lark cried, glee in his voice. "Thanks for the top tip, Seb."

"My pleasure," Sebastian replied. "I'm going to go get some coffee and maybe some of Brad's cinnamon rolls. I smelled them in your kitchen. Do you mind, Declan?"

"Not at all," the alpha replied. "I think I'll join ye."

"Me, too," Dixon stated. "See you later, guys."

After the trio said their good-byes, Lark stated, "Hold up there, Dermot. Let me get these stitches out, and then you can finish the rest."

Dermot stopped licking him. A moment later, Elroy felt an odd tugging sensation on his skin, and his stomach rolled a little. Breathing deeply, he focused on the low throb in his leg, instead.

That was easier to deal with.

After another moment, Dermot started licking him again.

These shifters are weird.

"There you go, baby," Dermot rumbled, squeezing his wrist. "Take a look."

Elroy girded up his courage and peered at his wrist. "Huh." All that was left was a pinkish-white scar. It ran from the fleshy area near his thumb up the inside of his wrist for a little over three inches. "Wow." Elroy wiggled his fingers, pleased to find it pain-free. Grinning at Dermot, he murmured, "Thank you."

"Anything for you, my mate," Dermot told him. Then he leaned toward him and pecked his lips to Elroy's. "Besides, I find your blood tastes delicious."

Recalling the claiming bite Dermot had given him, Elroy

chuckled. "That makes sense."

"All right," Lark called, redrawing their attention. "Let's take a look at your leg." The short doctor smirked at them. "Too bad the same technique can't be used to heal broken bones, huh?"

Elroy nodded, silently agreeing.

After thirty minutes, Lark proclaimed that Elroy was healing well.

"So, what the hell are the pain pills you have me on?" Elroy asked as he took a pair of crutches from Lark. "They're damn powerful."

"It's a medication I created with another scientist for shifters. Their metabolism burns too fast for any human meds to last for long," Lark told him. "They have to take two in order for them to work, but at least they do."

"You created them?" Elroy felt a slither of unease work through him. "Are they safe?"

Lark smiled, obviously catching on to his concern. "I would never give any of my pack something that was potentially harmful." He lifted his hands in placation while going into what exactly they were made of.

Within two sentences, Elroy didn't understand any of it.

Fortunately, Lark finished by telling him, "All ingredients are natural plant derivatives and are completely non-addictive. No man-made chemicals. Please know that you're completely safe."

Blowing out a breath, Elroy gripped the handles of the crutches. "Okay." He had to have faith that the doctor knew what he was doing, after all. "So. How do I use these things?"

After Lark explained how to use the crutches—which he could utilize now that he had both hands—Elroy slowly made his way out of the room. Dermot followed behind, his gaze ever watchful. When they reached the stairs, his lover insisted on going in front of him.

Elroy appreciated that. He made it down the stairs without mishap and settled into one of the dining room chairs. Dermot immediately helped him place his leg on a second chair, elevating it.

"So, ye said yer friends were coming by at eleven-thirty," Declan commented as he set a steaming mug before him. "How do ye like yer coffee?"

Fighting back a cringe, Elroy stared at the drink. He wondered if he could refuse a cup of coffee from the alpha of the shifters. Would that be rude? He didn't want to make his lover look bad.

"Damn, should have mentioned that, Alpha." Dermot took the decision away from him and picked up the mug. "I'll take it. Elroy doesn't drink coffee."

"Ye don't?" Alpha Declan appeared surprised but not offended.

Thank god.

Elroy shook his head. "Just never acquired the taste for it."

"A man after my own heart," someone rumbled from Elroy's left. He spotted a tall, slightly heavy-set man striding into the room. His steel-gray hair had been pulled away from his high forehead and into a ponytail. The man's black eyes twinkled. "You like tea? I know the alpha-mate keeps a variety of kinds here for me." Then he reached out a hand. "I'm Doctor Gordon Digby. Psychiatrist." Gordon pointed over his shoulder at a huge blond. "My mate, Detective Grady Stryker. He and his detective buddy Lyle are gonna find out who's causing trouble in your life."

Upon hearing his name, Grady turned and lifted his mug of coffee in greeting. "Hey, man," he mumbled around his mouthful of cinnamon roll.

"I'm never going to remember everyone," Elroy whispered, feeling more than a little overwhelmed.

"Don't worry about it," Dixon stated, placing two mugs before him. "There won't be a test." Grinning, he pointed to each in turn. "Earl Grey or Moroccan Mint? There are plenty of other flavors, too. Just say the word."

Reaching for the Moroccan Mint, Elroy met Dixon's gaze. "Thank you."

Dixon nodded, picked up the Earl Grey, and handed it to Gordon. "Yep. I like Black Dragon Pearl myself."

Just like that, Elroy found himself relaxing. After he'd taken a sip of his tea, he recalled Declan's question. "Oh, my friends did say eleven-thirty, but Camilla has a bad habit of showing up about fifteen to twenty minutes early."

Declan chuckled. "Good to know. I'll go start the grill." He left through a sliding glass door.

Elroy turned to Dermot, who was putting sugar in the cup of coffee. "Is it okay to ask what he's grilling?"

"Probably a little of everything. Steaks, burgers, brats," Dermot told him, licking his lips. "Your friends have any dietary restrictions we should know about? Allergies?"

Shaking his head, Elroy felt his stomach rumble. He was ready for some of all of that. Then he spotted Sebastian drinking from a mug and remembered him saying he was going to get a cup of coffee.

"Vampires eat real food?" Elroy blurted out the question, then slapped his hand over his mouth. With a groan, he grumbled, "I swear it's the meds messing with my brain to mouth filter."

Sebastian chuckled, joining him at the table. He sat down across from him. Over the next thirty minutes, he explained about vampires.

CHAPTER TEN

When the doorbell rang, Dermot clenched his hand around the coffee mug handle. His heart rate spiked a little, and he forced himself to take a deep calming breath. He knew who would be on the other side of the door.

Pack did not ring the bell.

Declan had an open-door policy during the day. If it was evening, the person would call first.

That means it's Elroy's friends. Time to make a good impression. Assuming they don't recognize me.

Dixon rounded the table, heading for the kitchen. As he passed, he rested his hand on the back of Dermot's neck. For just an instant, he squeezed, offering silent encouragement. Then Dixon was in the kitchen making himself another cup of tea.

"Want more, Elroy?" the beta called.

"Uh, yes, please," Elroy replied. Then his attention drifted toward the archway leading to the front room. "Hey, guys. Glad you could make it."

Camilla paused and took in the pale blue cast on his leg before letting out a soft cry and rushing toward Elroy.

It took every ounce of self-control Dermot possessed to stop himself from getting between them. Instead, he watched as Elroy's friend threw her arms around his mate's neck and hugged him. Hearing Elroy grunt, then hiss, he clenched his free hand in a fist.

His wolf growled in the back of his mind.

"Hey, Camilla," Elroy greeted. "Easy does it, huh?" His

mate urged his friend to unwind her arms. "Don't jostle the leg. It's only been a few days." When Camilla's brown eyes took on a hurt look, Elroy took her hands in his. "It's good to see you. Thanks for coming."

"Well, of course, I would come see you," Camilla stated. She glanced around at all the people before leaning close and whispering, "Gotta make sure you're actually here of your own free will."

Dermot knew that if he hadn't been a shifter, he wouldn't have heard her whispered words. Hell, so did probably every paranormal in the room, although the conversations didn't cease. For the most part, everyone began filtering out of the kitchen and dining area, probably to offer the illusion of privacy.

Schooling his expression, Dermot pretended he hadn't, although it pissed him off. He reminded himself that she was just being a protective best friend.

"Of course, I am," Elroy told her with a smile and nod. Then he turned his head and grinned. "Hey, Bart. Since you're only five minutes early, I'm going to guess that was down to you."

Bart laughed good-naturedly as he held out his hand. "Yeah. I wasn't ready when Camilla came to pick me up."

"You let Camilla drive you?" Elroy seemed surprised.

The brown-haired male shrugged his shoulders, but he scented just a smidge from embarrassment. "Well, Laura needed to take Nate to the doctor for a check-up on his wrist, and Mark was at a job, so I loaned her my car."

While the names meant nothing to Dermot, Elroy obviously understood. He nodded in sympathy. "How is Nate doing, anyway?" Then Elroy turned his attention on him. "Laura is his sister. Nate is his nephew, and he sprained his wrist on Saturday. Mark is the husband and father." Once Dermot nodded, Elroy refocused on Bart, who wore a smirk and was looking at Dermot.

"He's doing just fine," Bart stated, although his gaze didn't stray from Dermot. Then he held out his hand. "And you must be Florence Nightingale. I'm Bart Kovmar."

Dermot chuckled under his breath as he took Bart's hand. "Dermot Reever," he replied, shaking Bart's hand briefly. "Nice to meet you. Very happy you bailed, and now I know why."

Bart offered a sheepish look. "Glad it worked out for my buddy here." Then he indicated a red-faced Camilla. "This is my girlfriend, Camilla Hudson, who also happens to be Elroy's best friend."

"Girlfriend?" Camilla huffed, pinning Bart with an accusing stare. "After you throw me under the bus like that?"

"I'll make it up to you, sweetheart," Bart all but purred into her ear.

Camilla's face took on an even deeper hue of red, but she gamely replied, "You better, mister." Then she turned and held out her hand to Dermot. "Camilla Hudson."

Dermot took it and shook. "Nice to meet you, Camilla. Any friends of Elroy's and all that."

After they released, Camilla cocked her head. "You look really familiar. Have we met before?"

Shit.

Praying Camilla wouldn't place him, Dermot shook his head. "Not likely. I just moved to Stone Ridge a couple of months ago."

"Huh. You must just have one of those faces." Then Camilla turned her attention to Elroy, clapping her hands together. "Look. As your bestie, you know I have to ask." She glanced at Dermot again, then turned to Elroy.

Elroy grinned widely. "If you're about to ask me if this is Florence Nightingale effect, where the only reason I think I like him is because he saved my life, then no. That's not it."

"Are you sure?" Camilla turned to Dermot. "No offense."

"None taken," Dermot replied, smiling. "I know you're just trying to take care of your buddy, especially since you and Bart are the only people he considers family."

Camilla's blonde eyebrows shot up. "You told him about your family?" She sagged into the chair on the other side of where Elroy had his leg propped up. "Okay. Not Florence Nightingale effect then."

Bart settled beside her and rested his hand over Camilla's on the table.

Elroy grinned, pointing between them. "Soooo..." He waggled his eyebrows. "About damn time, guys. You've been pining over each other for the better part of four months."

Both their lips parted, obviously surprised by that announcement.

Shaking his head, Elroy reached over and took Dermot's hand, saying, "I thought I was going to have to shove them into an elevator and cut the power to the building, so they'd finally talk."

"Damn it, Elroy," Camilla shrieked. "How come you never said anything?"

Dermot barely managed to keep from rubbing his ear.

That human has a set of lungs on her, and damn, she is dramatic.

Dermot hoped it was only the strange situation.

Elroy sighed as he shook his head. "You both swore me to secrecy. Which of you should I have betrayed?"

The pair glanced between each other, then back at him.

"Okay," Camilla conceded while Bart muttered, "Point taken."

Dixon appeared with a fresh mug of tea for Elroy. "Here ya go, man." Offering a small smile to Bart and Camilla, he greeted, "Good to see you under better circumstances. Can I get you a drink?"

"Martini, three olives," Camilla requested.

The corners of Bart's lips twitched. "A cup of coffee is just fine."

Dixon didn't bat an eyelash at either request. "Coming right up." Turning, he headed toward the hall leading to the study, probably to make the lady's drink first.

"Keys, sweetheart." Bart held out his free hand and wiggled his fingers.

"Thanks." Camilla handed them over without question. She met Elroy's gaze squarely. "What? It's been a damn stressful six days, and I, for one, am ready to cut loose. I don't care if it is before noon."

Elroy chuckled. "No judgment, Cam. If I weren't on meds, I'd join you." He pointed at his cast, which made the comment self-explanatory.

"So, tell me all about your adventure," Camilla ordered.

Over the next few minutes, Elroy shared the altered version with his friends.

"Does everyone want to come outside?" Alpha Declan called. "Meat is done, and I believe all the sides have been set out here." Then he focused on Camilla and Bart. "Welcome to me home. Good to see ye again."

"Hi, Ranger McIntire," Camilla greeted. "Thank you for having us."

Declan grinned. "I'm off duty, Camilla. Declan is fine." Then he beckoned. "Chow's on."

Dermot stood, then carefully helped Elroy to his feet. Once he was certain his mate was steady, he released him. He grabbed both their mugs in one hand, keeping his other free in case Elroy needed assistance, and followed his lover onto the back deck.

"Careful on the planks, my mate," Dermot murmured, gripping Elroy's upper arm when he saw him wobble a little. The rubber tip of one crutch had wedged a little into a knothole. "Let's go to the chaise lounges to your left."

Elroy nodded and headed that way without comment.

Once Dermot had made certain Elroy was settled, his cup of tea on the nearby low table and a throw pillow under his leg, he pressed a kiss to his lips. "What would you like to eat, Elroy?"

"Can I get a small piece of steak as well as a brat," Elroy requested, smiling up at him. "And some chips or whatever is over there. I'm not picky."

"You got it." Dermot pecked his mate's lips again before heading away.

His shifter hearing allowed him to hear Camilla murmur, "My mate? What's that mean?"

Dermot winced at his slip.

Elroy chuckled. "Term of endearment, like baby or sweetheart." Before Camilla could ask another question, he told her, "When I called Richmond, he actually tried to get me to come in today. Can you believe it?" Snorting, Elroy added, "I quit on the spot. It was so damn satisfying."

Camilla laughed. "I bet."

"Wish I had guts to do that," Bart commented with a sigh. "But I need my bank teller job too much."

Dixon neared Dermot, heading toward Elroy and his friends. "How's he holding up?" the beta asked softly, pausing.

"Really good, I think, all things considered," Dermot told his beta. "He's staying with me while things get sorted, so it'll give me time to convince him to move in permanently." After a glance over his shoulder, Dermot added, "And he already quit his job."

Grinning, Dixon nodded. His pale blue eyes twinkled. "Glad to hear it." Then he lifted the beverages he held. "I'll get these to 'em." Except, Dixon didn't move. Instead, he murmured, "Camilla made it seem like she might have recognized you. Think it'll cause problems?"

When Dixon had joined their pack a couple of years ago,

Dermot had worried how the dominant wolf shifter would fit in. As time passed, he'd seen the way the beta, while a bit aloof, worked hard to learn his duties, catching on fast. Now, he handled everything Shane had with a quiet, solid presence that set pack-members at ease.

Dixon was also damn observant.

Dermot shrugged. "I'm really not sure. I'll ask Elroy to let me know if she makes any more comments about me."

After one last nod, Dixon moved on.

Making his way to the food, Dermot fulfilled his mate's food request.

"I'd like to go back to my apartment to inspect everything."

Upon hearing Elroy's quiet comment, Dermot froze. His hands were halfway to his mouth, and he'd been poised to take a big bite of his burger. He slowly lowered it as he arched a questioning brow at his mate.

"Camilla said the door had been busted in," Elroy told him, rubbing his hands over the fabric of the jeans he wore. They'd cut the left leg up the side nearly to his underwear so they could maneuver them over his cast, since Elroy hadn't wanted to wear sweat shorts to meet Dermot's alpha. "All my files were ransacked in my home office, just like they were strewn all over my car."

Dermot nodded slowly, thinking quickly. His heart thudded wildly in his chest. He nearly physically ached that he wouldn't be able to take his mate, but he couldn't show his face in Colin City.

"When were you thinking of going?" Dermot asked softly.

Meeting his gaze through his lashes, Elroy stated, "Tomorrow. Camilla offered to pick me up."

I just bet she did.

Dermot glanced at the slightly plump blonde woman who was leaning back against Bart in the chaise lounge they shared. He spotted the way her eyes were slightly narrowed as she eyed him over the rim of her martini glass. Even knowing she was up to something, Dermot would never deny his mate.

Refocusing on Elroy, Dermot picked up his hand. He threaded their fingers together and held his gaze steady. "I understand this is important to you, so it's important to me, too." After lifting Elroy's fingers to his lips, Dermot kissed his knuckles lightly before lowering them again. "But you and your safety is important, too. I know Camilla would do her best to help you if whoever is after you found you at your apartment." He turned his attention to Elroy's friend. "And I mean no offense to you, but I don't think you could protect him."

"So, does that mean you're not going to let him go?" Camilla asked. Her tone turned a little accusatory. "You know, he doesn't need your permission."

"Camilla," Elroy chided.

Leaning forward, Camilla frowned. "No, this is exactly the kind of shit Kyle used to pull. He just said you couldn't go, Elroy." Her brown eyes flashed with mistrust as she scowled at Elroy. "I won't let you get entangled with another abusive asshole, no matter how much you hate that I'm interfering."

"I didn't say Elroy couldn't go," Dermot countered, keeping his voice soothing.

"Yes, you did," Camilla claimed. "Kyle used to control your movements, too. He always wanted to know where you were going and who you were with. He—"

"Will you let me finish?" Dermot asked, cocking his head.

"No, I—" Camilla began.

At the same time, Elroy started, "Camilla, please calm down. This is different. Dermot is—"

Even as Dermot felt warmed and proud that his mate was sticking up for him, it was Bart's actions that he appreciated the most. Camilla's new boyfriend slapped his hand over her mouth as he clutched her close to his body. Dipping his head, he whispered into her ear.

"Hear him out, sweetheart. Please?" Bart nuzzled his nose along her cheek as he continued, "It took us so long to get together because we didn't communicate. Let's learn from that, huh?" After a peck to Camilla's neck, Bart added, "Let the man speak."

Although Camilla's expression appeared mutinous, she relented.

Dermot turned and swept his gaze over the still-crowded deck. Spotting the shifter he wanted, he called for him.

"What's up, Dermot?" The huge blond Bengal tiger shifter lowered his bulk into a nearby chair before taking a swig of his beer.

"Elroy, you met Detective Grady Stryker earlier this afternoon," Dermot stated before pointing at the other pair. "These are his good friends, Camilla and Bart."

Holding out a fist, Grady leaned toward Elroy. After his mate had bumped it with his own, the cat shifter nodded at the other pair. Grady leaned back in his chair.

"Thanks for calling me over, Dermot," Grady stated, although he was watching the humans. "Me and Lyle took a look at the files the Colin City boys compiled. We plan to take it over. The paperwork is already in the works." Then Grady focused on Elroy. "I'd like to take you to your apartment and have you walk through the place. See if anything is missing. I'm gonna warn ya...it's a disaster." Shaking his head, Grady rumbled, "Someone has a hard-on for ya and not the kind I think you want."

Smiling at Elroy, Dermot held his mate's gaze when his human stated, "You already knew he was going to take me, didn't you?"

Dermot winked. "I had a pretty damn good idea."

CHAPTER ELEVEN

"You're a shifter, too, right?" Elroy asked, glancing at the six-foot-three blond driving the truck.

"I am," Grady replied.

"What kind?" Upon seeing the detective's arched brow, he realized how presumptuous that could be and hurriedly added, "I'm sorry. Is it not okay to ask that?"

The corners of Grady's lips kicked up a little. "You can ask, but only friends and never if a human is around that doesn't know about us." Then he lifted a hand, stalling Elroy's next question. "And if you don't know for sure the human knows about us, just assume he or she does *not*. Okay?"

"Err on the side of caution," Elroy murmured, nodding. "Got it."

"Exactly." Reaching over, Grady squeezed his upper arm in a friendly way before returning his hands to the wheel. "And I'm a Bengal tiger."

Elroy let out an unmanly *eep* that he would forever deny. Staring at Grady, who was grinning broadly, he groaned. Of course with the dude's superior hearing, he'd heard it.

Clearing his throat, Elroy eyed the man. "Wow. Okay. A Bengal tiger."

"Yep." Grady sounded damn proud of that fact, too.

And well he should be. Tigers are badass.

After remaining quiet for a minute, Elroy formulated his next question. "So, if you don't mind my asking, how did a tiger shifter end up with a wolf pack? Adopted or something?"

Grady chuckled deep in his throat as he shook his head. "Naw. Long story short, Declan helped me transfer here from another state to track down a rogue shifter skirting his territory." Smiling, he rolled one shoulder in a half-shrug. "Honorary member, same as my mate."

"Gordon," Elroy recalled. "Uh, is he a wolf, then?"

Again, Grady shook his head. "Asian elephant."

"Gee-zus!" Gaping, Elroy shook his head. Upon managing to snap his mouth shut, he swallowed hard. "Wow." Cocking his head, he asked, "Are those the ones with the big ears and broad heads or the small ears and narrower heads?"

"Small ears and narrower heads, actually." Grady glanced his way a second, appearing impressed. "Do a lot of reading, I'm guessin'."

"When I'm running on the treadmill, I listen to a lot of books on tape," Elroy admitted before frowning at his casted leg. "Gonna be a while before I can do that."

"A few weeks at most, since you're bonded with Dermot. You movin' in with him permanent?"

"Um." Elroy didn't know how to answer that, ratcheting up his tension. Of course, all that did was increase the throb in his leg, since he'd flexed the muscles.

Reaching over again, Grady gripped his nape. He massaged lightly.

To Elroy's surprise, his tension faded.

Huh.

"Relax, man. Shifters do things fast. It's just the way we're wired."

Elroy nodded. "Dermot talked about that. Your instinct to please and care for."

"Exactly," Grady confirmed. "We can't please and care for our mate if they're not even in the same town." He flashed a knowing grin Elroy's way. "Don't fight the pull, buddy. Move in with him and put you both out of your miseries."

Heaving a sigh, Elroy fell silent. He stared out the window.

Trees mingled with the occasional house zipped by out the window, but he didn't focus on them. Elroy had too much on his mind.

"So, subject change, then." Grady broke into Elroy's thoughts. "Your apartment. Whatever you're expecting, it's worse."

Elroy grimaced. "Worse?" He'd thought they would have tossed all his papers about again, so what could be worse. "Like broken furniture and smashed dishes worse?"

Nodding, Grady told him, "There is that, but also other stuff." His lips pinched into a thin line. "Like someone dumped soiled cat litter and feces on your clothes worse."

"Gross," Elroy whispered. "Damn it."

"Yeah. Sorry. I'm a cat and can't imagine ever doing that, even to my worst enemy." Snorting, Grady added, "Not that I have any enemies, per se. My enemies, I just kill."

Staring wide-eyed at the shifter, Elroy commented, "But aren't you a detective?"

Grady arched one brow. "Yeah. So?" When Elroy just continued to stare, the cat shifter scoffed. "Ah, I see. Well, you have to consider that *my* enemies would either also be a shifter, or they would be some asshole trying to kill me for being a shifter." Shaking his head, Grady stated, "Either way, not someone I'm going to show mercy to."

"There are people out there trying to kill you because you're a shifter?"

Well, damn.

Nodding once, Grady pointed out, "There is always one faction or another trying to kill those different than themselves. It's been like that all throughout history."

"Ah, true."

Humans were not known as a tolerant species once a group formed together. Individuals, often, yes. But in a group, they turned into sheep. They would do whatever the shepherd told them to do.

"So, we'll go in, try to hold our noses, and you can mosey around and see if anything jumps out at you," Grady offered. "I understand wanting to check on your stuff, but if you want to forget it later, talk to Seb."

Just the idea of asking a vampire to wipe something from his mind scared the shit out of him. He never wanted someone inside his brain with him. His own thoughts were enough. Besides, if he saw something so horrible he wished he hadn't seen it, why would he force another person, even a vampire, to have to see it.

So glad I'm bonded with a shifter and not a vampire.

According to Sebastian, when a vampire bonded with their beloved—their term for mates—they forged a mind-link. They could talk to each other telepathically. While cool in theory, how were you supposed to hide things—like Christmas presents or surprise parties?

There's a thought.

"Do you guys celebrate holidays? Like give each other birthday or Christmas presents?"

"A lot of couples start out doing that, but after a few decades, it normally falls by the wayside," Grady answered, clearly being honest.

"That's too bad."

Grady drove into his apartment's lot and parked. After he'd shut off the engine, he turned and faced him. "You have to understand, Elroy. We're around for a long time." His smile turned understanding. "Eventually, it gets to be tough finding something unique for a partner or something they don't already have."

Elroy nodded slowly. "I guess it gets that way with any partner, huh?"

"Sometimes." Then Grady pushed open his door. "Stay there. I promised Dermot that I'd help you in and out. I don't want you falling."

While Elroy felt a little annoyed that Dermot had forced

Grady into such a promise, he sort of appreciated it, too. He was still getting used to the crutches. His balance was improving, but he wasn't certain he could slide out of a large pick-up truck, quite yet.

Grady opened the passenger door, then took the crutches and rested them against the truck bed. "One hand on my shoulder," he ordered as he placed one of his own on Elroy's right hip. He took his right hand with his other. "Take your time. Swing around, then slide out. Keep your weight on me. I won't be offended." Then Grady winked. "I'm mated. You're not my type."

Elroy snorted as he carefully maneuvered his way out of the truck. He appreciated the levity, considering he had to practically slide down the bigger man's body. Finally, Elroy got his right foot under him and balanced between Grady's shoulder and the door.

"Here's your crutches, El," Grady offered, helping him onto them. "Let's go see what we can find." Then he grabbed a couple of boxes from the bed of his pick-up. "These are for just in case you find something salvageable that you want to take."

The way Grady said salvageable didn't leave Elroy with much hope.

Just damn.

Hobbling across the foyer, Elroy paused at the mailboxes. He dug into his pocket, then handed his keys to Grady. "Wanna toss my mail into one of those boxes?"

"Sure can." Grady did as good as his word.

Elroy moved to the elevator and punched the up button.

Standing next to him, Grady groaned under his breath. "Sorry," he mumbled upon spotting Elroy's questioning look. "I hate enclosed spaces. Too much like a cage."

Having never considered that, Elroy wondered if Dermot felt the same way. He'd seen him hesitate in front of elevators in the courthouse a time or two. Plus, the man seemed to frequent the stairs.

Another reason they'd never run into each other.

Upon reaching the fourth floor, Elroy crutched his way down the hall, Grady leading the way. The detective pulled the crime scene tape off the door, then used Elroy's key to unlock it. He turned the knob and pushed open the door, heading inside.

The stench hit Elroy before he'd even entered. Just as Grady had warned, the place smelled of cat piss and feces. He grimaced as he stood in the doorway and slowly panned his gaze around the room.

Elroy's apartment wasn't large. He hadn't needed it to be. It was a two-bedroom, one-bath space with a small kitchen and dining area. The living space was a good size, however.

Every surface seemed to be covered in something. Paperwork littered the floor, and some of it appeared discolored as if it had been soaked in something but had since dried. Broken dishes were strewn across the dining room floor, and even a couple of chairs had lost their legs. Elroy thought someone had taken a razor blade to his sofa's cushions.

"My god," Elroy whispered, moving forward a few steps, only to pause again. All the doors were open, and he could see into his bedroom, his office, and his bathroom. All three were a mess. "Why?"

"I'm sorry, Elroy." Grady sounded so damn sincere, and his blue eyes sparkled with sympathy. "I told Dermot you shouldn't come, that he should spare you this, but he said you'd want to see it."

Elroy nodded. "He was right." Turning toward his office, he took a step. "Did my laptop survive?"

There were pictures on it that Elroy really wanted.

"No!" a familiar voice barked.

Before Elroy could turn, he was shoved forward. Only

Grady's lunge and arms around him kept him from face-planting on the dirty floor. Once Elroy was straight and steady again, Grady helped him face his attacker.

"Emerson," Elroy murmured. He couldn't help the quake in his voice upon seeing the gun in his brother's hand, and he recognized it as his own, stolen from his car. "Wh-What are you doing here?"

Instead of answering him, Emerson stated, "*I* have your laptop. You're going to change your last will and testament before I kill you."

"Well, that sure ain't much incentive," Grady drawled, sounding very hick-like. "Now, why on earth would my sweet Elroy do that?" As he spoke, he slung his arm loosely around his waist.

Elroy wasn't certain what the detective was doing until he felt the man angle in front of him ever-so-slightly.

Right. Protection.

"You're going to will gramma's inheritance to me," Emerson demanded. "If you don't, I'm gonna kill your boyfriend, too." He curled his lip and sneered. "Fucking faggots ruining the earth."

"Well, now. That ain't very nice—" Grady began to drawl.

"I can't, Emerson," Elroy burst out. "Please, don't hurt him."

Elroy didn't want to see anyone get hurt by his psychotic family, even an acquaintance. Except, when he tried to move forward, Grady's arm—which had seemed loose—wouldn't allow him to. The shifter had one hell of a grip on him.

"If you give me what I want, I'll let your faggot partner go," Emerson claimed. From the crazy look in his younger brother's eyes, Elroy didn't know if he believed him. "Come on, big bro. Do the right thing."

"As if you would have any idea about doing the right thing," a sultry tenor toned. "Another gay basher. Gods, I do hate them."

"What the—" Emerson began to turn.

Grady released Elroy, going for his gun.

Whoever stood behind Emerson wrapped one arm around his brother's torso. With his other, he grabbed Emerson's wrist and twisted. His brother screamed as the gun fell from his grip. Then the stranger shoved Emerson face-first into the wall. By the time his brother managed to sit up, the guy had pulled a gun from somewhere—since Emerson's was at the man's braced feet—and was pointing it at his downed would-be attacker.

"Lower your weapon, now!" Grady boomed in an authoritative voice. "Do it, man."

The stranger, who had black hair and a wide nose, shifted his grip and allowed the gun to swing around the trigger guard.

"As much as I appreciate a helping hand"—Grady eased forward a step, his own drawn weapon pointed at the floor between Elroy's felled brother and the stranger—"who are you?"

Tsking, a sly smile curved the guy's full lips. "You're welcome, Grady. Always happy to help a friend."

"D-Do you know this guy, Grady?" Elroy asked tentatively, glancing between them. He saw the stranger wink one blue eye at him. The detective, however, was staring in open-mouthed shock. "G-Grady?"

"*Jared*?" Grady's tone was incredulous.

The man's grin managed to broaden.

Taking advantage of the confusion, Emerson dove for his gun. The guy, Jared, responded instantly by kicking him in the face. He also once again leveled his weapon at him.

"Don't shoot him, Jared," Grady ordered even as he shoved his own weapon back into his holster. "I need the bastard alive."

Heaving a put-upon sigh, Jared lowered his weapon.

Grady surged forward and made swift work of slapping cuffs on Emerson. While holding onto his brother's cuffed wrists, he leveled another incredulous look Jared's way. Obviously, the tiger shifter had not expected to see him.

"What the hell are you doing here?"

Jared shrugged. "I was on my way through town, headed for Stone Ridge, when I spotted this yahoo sneaking into the building after you. Figured it could be fun to check it out."

Shaking his head, Grady reiterated, "No, but what are you *doing* here."

"Oh." Jared's grin this time appeared a little malicious. "I found Larson."

"Fuck me," Grady whispered, betraying the importance of that.

Laughing, Jared put his weapon away. "No, thanks."

CHAPTER TWELVE

"Something happened. Come here."

That was all Alpha Declan had told Dermot. He'd asked for more, but his alpha had replied, "Not over an unsecured line."

For that reason, Dermot drove hell-bent for leather toward Declan's lodge. When he took a turn too fast, his *Jeep*'s tires squealed. Realizing getting into an accident on the way to finding out what was going on would be a very bad thing, Dermot forced himself to slow down.

When Dermot arrived, relief slammed through him, almost making him lightheaded. Elroy stood on the porch between Declan and Grady. He looked a little pale, but other than that, he seemed fine.

Dermot turned off his engine. Leaving the keys in the ignition and the door open, he sprinted across the lawn. He took the steps two at a time, slowing just enough to where he didn't barrel into his lover.

"Elroy," Dermot purred into his human's neck. "My mate. Are you okay?"

"Nothing a little at-home painkillers wouldn't cure," Elroy whispered back.

Moaning upon hearing Elroy's teasing, Dermot nuzzled his neck. "As soon as possible."

Feeling Declan's hand on his neck, Dermot lifted his head. "We have a few things to discuss first, I'm afraid."

Dermot nodded. "Okay." He turned and asked Grady, "Take his crutches, will ya?"

As soon as Grady complied, Dermot swung Elroy into his arms and cradled him against his chest.

"I can walk, you know," Elroy stated, smirking up at him.

"I know, but I like holding you." Dermot pressed a gentle kiss to Elroy's lips. "I missed you."

Elroy's grin appeared almost shy. "I was only gone three hours."

"And that was three hours too long," Dermot declared, heading into the house.

A pair of men stood in the front room to his right. While he didn't recognize one, the other he did. "Enforcer Carson." He tipped his head in greeting. "Welcome back." Then the stranger's scent hit him, and recognition slammed into him. "Jared?"

"Yeah, I about had the same reaction," Grady told him, moving past him. "I mean, I *knew* he was good at disguises, but damn."

Jared tipped his head back and laughed. Then he began removing his facial prosthetics. There was a nose piece to broaden his own. He removed a thin layer of skin that had made each cheek appear fuller. His chin even had one that gave him a cleft.

Taking a wet cloth from Carson, Jared wiped down his face. He opened and closed his mouth a couple of times, stretching the skin of his cheeks. Then he wiped his face once more. After repeating that process two more times, Jared sighed and tossed the damp towel onto a side table where he'd been setting the prosthetics into a small case.

Finally, Jared grinned at everyone. "The hair will be black for a few days, yet." He turned and cupped Carson's jaw. "Missed you, Injun."

Growling, the big Native American wolf shifter dipped his head and sealed his mouth over Jared's.

"Oh, we get to see this again. Awesome," Dixon rumbled

drolly.

Jared and Carson broke their kiss, and Jared waggled his black eyebrows as he fixed his blue-eyed gaze on Dixon. "Admit it, Beta Dixon. You missed the show."

To Dermot's shock, Dixon tipped his head back and laughed.

Alpha Declan snorted, then crossed and wrapped Carson in a welcoming hug. "Welcome home, me friend." He eased away, still grinning widely. "I'd say I can't wait to hear about yer adventures, but traveling with this one here" — he ruffled Jared's hair, which was longer than Dermot had ever seen it, reaching a bit past his ears — "I'm not certain it's safe to hear."

"I'd never do anything to shame you, Alpha," Carson replied, dipping his head.

Cupping Carson's nape, Alpha Declan replied, "I know." Then he released the wolf shifter's nape and stepped away. "I hear there was an adventure at Elroy's, and ye have caught the man responsible for burgling Elroy's car and destroying his home." Declan's dark brows furrowed as he rested his hands on his hips. "At least the attempted murder charge will put him away for a while."

"I'll flag his name in the system," Jared claimed, crossing his arms over his chest. "If he has a hearing or will be released, we'll know about it."

"Who are they?" Elroy whispered.

Of course, everyone in the room heard it.

Alpha Declan grinned and pointed at the Native American first. "That is me head enforcer, Carson Angeni and his mate, Jared Templeton. They've been away for the last year and a half while the news of their deaths has been assimilated by the humans who knew them."

"They're in hiding for the next decade, like me," Dermot explained to him. "Their only contact will be with other pack-members or paranormals."

"You made an exception with Camilla and Bart," Elroy commented astutely. "To make me happy."

"Yes, I did," he confirmed.

"But we put safeguards in place," Alpha Declan reminded him. His gaze turned serious as he added, "And if either of yer friends make a comment about Dermot's deceased identity in reference to him, I do need ye to let me know."

Elroy nodded. "Yes, Alpha."

"When are you taking the contacts out?" Dixon asked Jared, peering down at him. "You with blue eyes is...wrong."

Jared chuckled. "Forgot I had them in." He pulled a contact case from the bag on the end table and quickly removed them. He blinked a few times, put a few eye drops into each eye, then turned back to Dixon, staring at the beta with his usual hazel-colored eyes and a big grin on his face. "Better?"

Dixon nodded once. "Yep."

Bowing deeply, Jared bumped his ass backward into Carson's crotch.

Dermot just knew he did it on purpose, since Carson popped him on one butt cheek, causing Jared to laugh.

"Good to be home?" Dermot asked, smiling at the pair's antics. Before Carson had found his slightly crazy mate, he'd been quiet, serious, and intense. While Dermot still thought he was uber-focused, now that drive was split between his pack and keeping his mate in line...sort of.

Carson nodded. "It is. Missed everyone." He pointed at Dermot with a circling finger. "Like you better with the facial hair and no piercings."

Elroy snorted. "Oh, he still has piercings."

Seeing Carson's eyebrows shoot up, Dermot laughed.

"Touché," Carson replied. Then he stepped forward and held out his hand. "Carson Angeni. Welcome to the pack."

While Carson and Elroy shook hands, Jared joined them. He smirked. "Don't get used to calling him that. We'll have new names soon enough." His provocative gaze swept down Carson's body, then back up again. "Maybe...Ahanu."

Carson frowned. "What?"

"It means *he laughs*," Jared deadpanned.

His mate's eyes just narrowed.

Jared shrugged. "How about Istu?"

Sucking in a harsh breath, Carson grumbled, "I'm afraid to ask."

Waggling his brows, Jared told him, "It means *sugar*."

"Oh, gods." Carson began scrubbing his hands through his hair, scratching his scalp. "This is going to be torture."

Elroy glanced between the pair, then blurted out, "How about Kajika?"

Both men turned to peer at him. Carson arched one brow in silent question.

After clearing his throat, Elroy revealed, "It means *walks without sound*." He shrugged. "Wolf shifter head enforcer." When no one said anything, Elroy hunched a little in Dermot's arms as he muttered, "Sorry. Just popped into my head."

"I like it," Carson declared, a smile curving his lips. "Thank you."

Elroy's tension melted out of him. "Uh, you're welcome."

Carson arched a brow as he pinned his focus on Jared.

Heaving a put upon sigh, Jared grumbled, "I suppose it will do...Kajika."

"Then I will be—" Jared began, but Carson cut him off with a kiss.

When Carson lifted his head, he declared, "*You* will not get to decide right now. The alpha is waiting, and we have much to discuss with him."

Dermot turned to see every member of the inner circle standing not too far away. He couldn't even say when they'd arrived. He and his mate had been too busy chatting with

Jared and Carson.

There were others there, too. Jared's buddy Raul crossed the room and wrapped his friend in a hug. The pair slapped backs twice, then separated, although they kept their heads together. They started talking about code and tracking signals and other hacker things that Dermot didn't understand.

"We have something very important to discuss, Jared." Alpha Declan's tone had taken on a decidedly hard edge. "Grady tells me ye claim to know where Larson is."

Sucking in a harsh breath in surprise, Dermot glanced between Jared and Carson. He knew Larson had been one of the wolves that participated in the Right for Beta Position challenge. He'd been disqualified. Then he'd orchestrated a kidnapping of Sara—the alpha's daughter—and an attempted bombing of Jared and Carson. After saving Sara, the pair had used the bomb to fake their deaths.

"We do, Alpha," Jared replied, suddenly serious. "Larson is in league with ex-Councilman Krakow. He was sent to win the beta position and infiltrate the pack." His tone turned deadly. "I believe we can use our knowledge of his whereabouts to help Shane clean up the council."

Growling softly under his breath, Alpha Declan asked, "How did ye learn of this?"

Jared's smile appeared anything but happy. "A little bird told me."

"Aaaahhhh." Alpha Declan nodded. He beckoned with a crooked finger. "This way, gentlemen."

Dermot was tempted to just follow. He'd never sat in on his inner circle's gatherings, however. Clearing his throat, he caught his alpha's attention.

Alpha Declan did his best to give him a kind smile. "Thank ye for comin' to get yer mate and for welcoming back Enforcer Carson and his mate." He turned his attention to Elroy. "I look forward to seeing more of ye, Elroy. Heal well, and I'm certain me mate will be contacting ye about check-ups."

"Thank you, Alpha Declan," Dermot stated, and Elroy parroted him.

Declan chuckled, then turned and followed the others down the hall.

Dermot knew he'd been dismissed, so he headed out the front door.

Before Dermot closed it, he heard Jared ask, "How come you never carry me like that, Injun?"

Carson growled. "Because you prefer to be carried like *this*."

Unable to help himself, Dermot turned and looked. Carson had swung Jared over his shoulder. His bronzed hand had clamped onto his chortling mate's ass. Like that, Carson carried Jared out of the front room.

Jared winked at them before they disappeared.

"Wow," Elroy murmured. "Are they always like that?"

"From what I've heard, yes."

"Jared's the one who stopped my brother, Emerson, from trying to shoot me or Grady."

Upon hearing that, Dermot almost dropped his lover. He caught himself just in time. After placing Elroy in the passenger seat, he rested his hands on either side of the frame.

"Please, explain."

Elroy did, sharing how Jared had shown up out of the blue.

"Gods, now I need to go back and thank him," Dermot muttered. "I didn't know."

"Guess he and Carson were taking different routes to keep Larson from figuring out they were heading back here," Elroy continued to explain. He shook his head. "Jared changed his looks and drove some beat-up *Pinto*, and Carson ran in wolf form. They managed to get back at about the same time."

Barking a laugh, Dermot shook his head. "I wish I could have seen that. Jared driving a *Pinto*." Seeing Elroy's confused look, he explained, "Jared is very much a car snob. Even living in the mountains for ten years, he still drove a *Porsche* just about everywhere."

Snickering, Elroy shook his head. Then he grabbed Dermot's hand and squeezed. "Thank him another time. I'm ready to go home."

"H-Home?" Hope sprang eternal, and Dermot felt his heart thud in his chest.

Elroy narrowed his eyes and nodded. "*Home*...with you."

Moaning, the need to claim his mate surging through him all over again, Dermot nodded. "*Home*."

Then Dermot closed Elroy's door and rushed around the hood of his *Jeep*. He clambered inside and cranked the engine. As he put the vehicle in gear, Elroy cried, "Wait."

Biting back a groan, Dermot turned to focus on Elroy.

"My crutches."

Shaking his head, Dermot turned his vehicle around and headed out. "I'll have someone bring them to us eventually." He grinned and swept a hungry once-over his mate. "You won't need them for a few days, anyway."

Elroy laughed, clearly catching his meaning.

Happy beyond measure, Dermot took Elroy home...where he intended to give his mate all the natural painkillers in the world...while in bed.

His heart hammering in anticipation, Dermot did exactly as he planned.

"Speaking of which," Krispin commented before knocking back the rest of his whiskey. "It's getting late. I'm going to head up. I'll have my phone on me if anything arises that needs my attention."

Basques nodded. He was on management duty that evening. They rotated it between the three of them, so no one ended up burned out.

"Have a good one, Kris," Ridger offered before sweeping his gaze over the lounge. "I don't see what I'm after in here, so I think I'll head to the dance club." He waggled his brows and licked his lips.

Chuckling, Basques patted Ridger on his shoulder. "Happy hunting, my friend."

Krispin paused, watching Ridger head out of the room. He knew what his buddy planned to do. His vampire second was looking for a little action so he could feed.

Turning back to Basques, Krispin asked, "I bet you don't miss that, do you?"

Basques shook his head, a warm smile creasing the features as a faraway light entered his eyes. "Definitely not."

A pang of jealousy churned in Krispin's gut, and he quickly squashed it. He didn't want Dloben, but he did want what his head enforcer had found. At over two hundred years old, he was getting a little tired of waiting.

And, yet, continue to wait, I shall.

Krispin headed out of the lounge and crossed to the elevator. Inserting a key card into the slot, he hit the button for floor thirteen. He and his inner circle lived on the first floor above the humans — first line of defense and secrecy.

The vampire covens' floors could only be accessed with a key card.

Once Krispin reached his suite, he headed straight for the bedroom, unbuttoning his suite jacket on the way. He tossed his wallet, keys, card, and phone on the nightstand. After that, he quickly stripped, placing his dirty clothes into the hamper.

Krispin took a short, hot shower, happy to wash off the stress of the day. After drying, he grabbed a pair of pale green lounging pants. He picked up his phone and keycard, slid his feet into a pair of house shoes, then left his suite.

The private elevator Krispin headed to could only be accessed by a select few, since it was the only one that reached the roof. Stepping inside, anticipation filled him. He inserted his keycard before tapping the button for the roof.

As soon as the door swished open, revealing the warm evening, Krispin inhaled deeply. The fragrance of flowers, earth, and bushes filled his senses. The trickle of the fountain reached his ears. Soft lights revealed the maze of the garden paths as well as the colorful plants.

Krispin smiled.

Stepping off the elevator, Krispin headed down a path to his right. His friend's assessment — rooftop oasis — really was accurate. He loved it up there.

Pausing at a storage closet set up against the wall of the greenhouse, Krispin pulled out his yoga mat. His penchant for yoga and meditation wasn't common knowledge in his coven. He liked to keep that little personal nugget to himself and a few trusted people—namely, Ridger, Basques, and now Dloben.

It wasn't that he was embarrassed by his nightly ritual. Instead, he just didn't care for the teasing he knew it would invite. What he got up to in private was his own business.

Placing the yoga mat on a grassy stretch near the fountain, Krispin stepped onto it and began his nightly routine. As he moved through different poses, focusing on his breathing and headspace, he felt the troubles of the day slip away. His mind cleared, and the muscles of his body warmed.

Perfect.

Krispin was just wrapping up his routine when an odd whooshing sound reached his sensitive ears. Cocking his head, he straightened and rested his hands on his hips. He narrowed his eyes and waited to see if it came again.

It did, accompanied by the unmistakable sound of flesh hitting flesh and a roar.

"What the hell?" Krispin peered around, searching for the source. "Who's fighting at my coven?"

To Krispin's shock, movement to his right drew his attention just in time to watch a large form slam into a trellis, wiping it out. The body continued to tumble, carving a trail of dirt and destruction. A blueberry bush went next, followed by a bed of daylilies. Finally, the brown-skinned form came to a stop beside a pecan tree.

Krispin started toward it warily. He spotted black wings, and realized he was staring at a gargoyle.

What the hell?

He was within twenty feet of the male when another gargoyle landed next to the fallen one. Instead of helping, the gray-hided gargoyle swung a black-clawed hand and flayed the skin of the brown gargoyle's back. Blood sprayed from the wound…hitting Krispin in the face and torso.

Licking his lips at it on reflex, Krispin discovered two

things at once.

My beloved just fell from the sky right in front of me, and some motherfucker is trying to kill him.

Hell no!

Screaming a battle cry, Krispin lunged. With his vampire speed, he easily reached the attacker between one heartbeat and the next. He sliced his claws through one black wing as he sank the claws of the other into the gargoyle's back, right about where the kidney should be.

The gargoyle belled and lunged forward, jumping away from Krispin. He pivoted and spread his thick arms and wide wings.

"Stay out of this, vampire," the male ordered.

"You landed on the roof of my coven house," Krispin stated. "No unsanctioned attacks will take place here. State your name and business."

No way was he going to tell the bastard of his discovery. He didn't know what was going on between the two males, but he wasn't going to allow him to hurt his beloved.

Sneering, the gargoyle stated, "As if you could stop me."

The male lunged forward, but Krispin was ready. He pivoted and swung, slicing his three-inch talons into the gargoyle's side. The male was clumsy, thinking his massive, six-foot-six frame gave him an advantage.

Krispin hadn't kept hold of his coven for one-hundred-fifty years with words alone. He'd been in his fair share of fights. He easily evaded the gargoyle's attempts to hit him, countering with blows to the creature's torso, thighs, and wings each time.

After Krispin's third slash to the gargoyle's wings, the other paranormal bellowed with rage as he lifted off the ground. At first, Krispin thought he would dive-bomb him or something. Instead, he flew away, yelling that it wasn't over.

Krispin watched the gargoyle until he was out of sight in the dark sky.

"Moron doesn't even know if he's being watched by a human," Krispin grumbled, shaking his head. "What the fuck?"

Then a low moan caught his attention, returning his focus to his downed beloved.

Rushing to the male's side, Krispin took in the flayed hide of his back and one wing. He grimaced as he knelt beside him. As much as he wished he could begin licking the wounds to seal them, he didn't know the male or what had brought him here.

But I will soon.

The fact that he hadn't woken, yet was cause for concern, too.

"Right, get my head out of my ass."

Krispin jumped to his feet and rushed back to his yoga mat. He grabbed his phone and dialed Basques's number. His enforcer picked up on the second ring just as Krispin dropped back to his knees beside the gargoyle.

"Hey, buddy," Basques greeted. "All's quiet here. No need to—"

"Shut up a sec," Krispin cut him off. "I need you to locate Ward and bring him and Dloben up to the roof. Ridger, too, if he's not with a donor."

"I'm on the move," Basques replied instantly, and the noise of the lounge disappeared from the background. "I'll bring everyone up as quickly as I can. What's going on?"

Unable to touch, Krispin threaded his fingers through the gargoyle's shaggy, dark-brown hair, pushing it away from his face. "My mate just fell from the sky. Literally."

"What the fuck?"

Krispin felt about the same. "He's a gargoyle. He was attacked, and he's injured. Unconscious. I was wondering if Dloben would recognize him."

"Damn, Kris," Basques muttered through the line. "Congrats, and don't worry. I'm sure he'll be fine." Then a laugh erupted from him.

"What?" Krispin didn't know what his buddy could find

funny about the situation.

"Guess you're stuck carryin' your offspring, just like me."

Krispin felt his gut twist and his ass clench. Gargoyles could get their male mates pregnant.

"Oh fuck."

About the Author

Charlie started writing fantasy when she was eight, and after stumbling onto her first erotic romance at age nineteen, she realized her true calling. She now focuses on writing gay erotic romance, normally of the paranormal variety, with heroes of all kinds. With the help and support of her husband, Charlie finally fulfilled one of her life-long goals…move to acreage with her horses. You can often find her curled up with her laptop and a cup of tea or glass of wine, creating her next adventure. Charlie enjoys exploring the mountains of her new Oregon home on horseback, 4-wheeler, or motorcycle.

She can be reached at ch.richards2010@yahoo.com
Or visit her at www.charlie-richards.com

www.ingramcontent.com/pod-product-compliance
Lightning Source LLC
Chambersburg PA
CBHW060641130626
46555CB00002B/905